the Wavering
Knife

the Wavering

Knife

Brian Evenson

FC2
NORMAL/TALLAHASSEE

Published by FC2 with support provided by Florida State University, the
Unit for Contemporary Literature of the Department of English at Illinois
State University, the Illinois Arts Council, and the Florida Arts Council of
the Florida Division of Cultural Affairs

Address all inquiries to: Fiction Collective Two, Florida State University,
c/o English Department, Tallahassee, FL 32306-1580

ISBN: Paper, 1-57366-113-9

Library of Congress Cataloging-in-Publication Data
Evenson, Brian, 1966-
The wavering knife : stories / Brian Evenson.—1st ed.
p. cm.
ISBN 1-57366-113-9 (pbk.)
I. Title.
PS3555.V326W38 2004
813'.54—dc22
2003020424

Cover Design: Victor Mingovits
Book Design: Tara Reeser

Produced and printed in the United States of America
Printed on recycled paper with soy ink

The author gratefully acknowledges the editors of the magazines in which these stories appeared. Special consideration is also due to the following individuals, in no particular order: Bradford Morrow, Vincent Standley, Ben Marcus, Alan Tinkler, John Yau, Samuel Delany, George Saunders, Chris Kennedy, Gary Lutz, and Joanna Howard. I am grateful to Glenna Luschei, Hilda Raz, Erin Flanagan, and the editors at *Prairie Schooner* for awarding "Virtual" the *Glenna Luschei Prairie Schooner Award*.

"White Square"	*Post Road*
"The Ex-Father"	*Salt Hill* and *Highway 14*
"The Intricacies of Post-Shooting Etiquette"	*The Chicago Review*
"Promisekeepers"	*American Literary Review*
"Calling the Hour" and "Müller"	*Conjunctions*
"Moran's Mexico"	*McSweeney's*
"The Wavering Knife"	*The Denver Quarterly*
"Virtual"	*Prairie Schooner*
"Barcode Jesus"	*The Southern Review*
"One Over Twelve," "House Rules," and "Garker's Aestheticals"	*Third Bed*
"The Prophets"	*Prophets and Brothers* (Rodent Press, chapbook)
"The Progenitor"	*Leviathan*
"The Gravediggers"	*The Quarterly*
"Body"	*Fetish: A Literary Anthology*
"The Installation"	*The Paris Review*

Table of Contents

...the fevered darkness of night in which words work, eating away at the skins with which realities surface in the sun...

—Alphonso Lingis, Foreign Bodies

We have fallen out of being, outside where, immobile, proceeding with a slow and even step, destroyed men come and go.

—Maurice Blanchot, The Writing of the Disaster

White Square

The black square on the table is meant to represent Gahern's estranged wife; it is presented as such at Gahern's request. The gray square beside it stands in for the black square's new husband, also presented as such at Gahern's request. Though Hauser has offered him the full gamut of shapes and colors, Gahern insists upon remaining unrepresented. Nothing stands in for him. When Hauser suggests to Gahern that the investigation might proceed more smoothly were a shape allowed to stand in for him as well, Gahern simply refuses to reply. *Perhaps a green rhombus?* suggests Hauser. Gahern asks to be returned to his cell.

The investigation, Hauser repeatedly reminds himself, is progressing poorly. Gahern will only speak when both the black square and the gray square are on the table before him. Even then he says little, if anything, of use. When questioned concerning the whereabouts of the gray and black squares, Gahern says nothing. He will not indicate whether these squares represent persons alive or dead. *These are meant to stand in for them, they are symbols*, is all he will indicate, gesturing to the squares. When Hauser hides the squares in his lap and asks Gahern where they have gone, Gahern only says, *They are in your lap*.

Such are the facts as Hauser has recorded them:

- Individuals represented by gray and black squares both disappeared, 12 October. Said individuals absent three months now.
- Said disappearance preceded by Gahern's own sudden disappearance, 17 August. When, 8 November, Gahern reappeared and returned to former workplace to request reinstatement, he cited his reason for being absent as *continued persecution by my estranged wife and her new husband*. Said persecution, he indicated to lathe foreman, had concluded, was not to be resumed.
- After Christmas, Gahern found to be living in black and gray squares' residence (Gahern's former residence before estrangement from black square), with both squares having disappeared. This last fact compelled Hauser, at Commissioner Torver's request, to open an investigation.

The additional information Hauser has amassed through interrogating Gahern is marginal at best. Hauser's investigation, Gahern insists, is a form of persecution somehow perpetrated by black and gray squares from a distance—their persecution of him has unexpectedly resumed. He is certain they will never leave him alone. He fled to escape them, came back only when he had taken steps to assure his escape. Now, he can see, he escaped nothing.

"What steps did you take to assure an escape?" asks Hauser.

"It is of the utmost importance," claims Gahern, "that I be provided a new identity and be allowed to leave the city immediately."

"Of course," says Hauser. "We will assign you a new identity: Rhombus, Green. Just answer a few questions first."

In Gahern's private world, Hauser thinks as he sits in stocking feet, a cup of hot water before him, *there is only one shape*. *Square*. There are, however, two colors. Or rather two shades— gray and black. Each of which admittedly might be described as a lightening or darkening of the other.

Through the window, through square panes of glass, he can see down into the central courtyard. The courtyard consists of eight rectangular slabs of concrete, of a slightly lighter gray than the gray square meant to represent the new husband. Beyond, he can see the even facade of the North wing of Branner B. Hauser's office is in the South wing of Branner B, a building designed by one Edouard Branner if a plaque on one marble corner of the building is to be believed. In his travels about the city, from crime scene to crime scene, Hauser keeps an eye open for Branner A, the precursor of Branner B. He has never seen it. Perhaps Branner A was torn down to make way for another building, perhaps even for Branner B. Whatever the crime that presents itself to him, Hauser's first question is always the name of the residence or residences attached to the crime.

Yet this crime is different. There is no crime scene to visit. He cannot ask his habitual question. Instead, it is just he and Gahern, in a narrow room, a table between. Only words. Or as now, just he himself, in his office, alone. Only thoughts.

One shape, he thinks. *Two shades.*

Why is it that Gahern will not take a shape and color to represent himself? Can I force him to accept a shape and color?

Was it prudent, wonders Hauser, *to have allowed this game of squares and shades to commence?*

"Shall we try again, Mr. Gahern?" asks Hauser. "Where were you during the month of October?"

"Fleeing the persecution of the following," says Gahern, and reaches out to finger first the black squares, then the gray square.

"Of what did said persecution consist?"

"They constantly disturbed me," says Gahern. "They appropriated my residence, interrupted my sleep, impeded me on my path to work, insulted me, interfered with my operations on the lathe in my place of employ—"

"—Yet, Mr. Gahern, curiously enough, I have a sheet of paper before me which claims that the reverse of what you say is true. On seven separate occasions complaints were filed against you by your ex-wife and her new husband, the last culminating in a restraining order."

"This too is part and parcel of their persecution of me."

"Where are they, Mr. Gahern? What have you done with them?"

"These are meant to stand in for them," says Gahern, gesturing to the squares.

"I'm afraid that doesn't answer my question," says Hauser.

Gahern folds his arms, tightens his lips.

Hauser receives a telephone call. It is Commissioner Torver. *How is the investigation?* Torver wants to know.

"It seems to have become a sort of geometry problem," says Hauser.

"Yes," says Torver, "so I hear. Or a child's game. Do you think it wise, Hauser? Shall I step in so we can have a word?"

Hauser assents and recradles the headpiece, awaits Torver's arrival. As he waits, he looks at the square panes of glass in the window. *Surely*, he thinks, *I will be reprimanded*.

He realigns the already aligned piles of paper on his desk, picks up the gray and black squares. *If Torver were a square*, he is starting to wonder as Torver enters, *what color square would he be?*

Yet, he suspects in looking at the man's face, in watching his lips move, that a square would not be the proper shape for Torver.

Hauser has two days and then the investigation will be taken from him, Torver seems to be saying. The gist of his words comes to Hauser as if from a distance. *Like Gahern*, thinks Hauser, fingering the squares, *I myself prefer to remain unrepresented.* Apparently Hauser's methods are most unorthodox, but Torver is willing to let him extend said unorthodox methods for a short period. Hauser must not let him down. *Perhaps a rectangle*, Hauser thinks of Torver, but soon discards this in favor of a simple oval. By the time he has settled on a dirty white for the color, the simple oval has finished its admonishments and is just going, leaving Hauser alone to wonder what the Commissioner's shape and shade signify.

Perhaps, thinks Hauser, *I could produce a series of squares moving in almost indiscernible increments from black to gray and substitute them in consecutively for each square on the table.* After a number of careful substitutions, the black square would wither to gray and the gray square would have ripened to black. Gahern might realize something was happening, but perhaps would not understand what. Suddenly he would perceive that the square he thought gray was black and the square he thought black, gray.

And what, Hauser wonders, regarding his reflection in a pane of glass, *would be the point of that?*

Anything could happen, one of them suggests, either him or his reflection, perhaps both.

But nothing significant ever does.

Something could.

You have two days. You haven't time to experiment.

Perhaps, one of them thinks, *both squares could be gradually changed until they are nothing but two pieces of slick white cardstock, squares of light shining up from the tabletop.*

He closes his notebook, turns each square face down. Time has passed. He has learned nothing. Gahern is still there, just on the other side of the table. Unrepresented, still himself. *I, too*, Hauser insists, *remain unrepresented.* He holds his hand before his face, assures himself it is still a hand.

He watches the hand remove a cigarette from a pack, extend it toward Gahern.

Cigarette? he hears his mouth offer. He knows that the voice he hears in his head sounds different to him than it must sound to Gahern, listening outside the head that speaks. Who is to say who hears the voice correctly?

Gahern takes the cigarette, tucks it into his breast pocket. "You look tired," he says.

"What do you know about Branner A?" asks Hauser.

"Who?"

"Not who," says Hauser. "What. And A, not B."

"I don't know anything," says Gahern. "I don't even know what you're talking about."

"Look," says Hauser. "Let's forget everything. I don't care what you did with the squares. I'm willing to forget all that. Just tell me where to find Branner A."

Gahern does not answer. Instead he regards his fingernails. To Hauser, from the other side of the table, the fingernails appear to be normal. There is no reason that he can see for anyone to be looking at them. Yet he cannot stop looking.

Hauser's time all but gone, his methods failed, he has let Torver down or is about to. *A final effort*, his reflection tells him, *gird yourself.*

He brings in a piece of paper, blank, places it on the table between the black and gray squares. He sits across the table from Gahern, watching him.

He lets nearly an hour slip by without speaking. He looks at Gahern's face, trying to will it into a simpler shape.

He takes a pencil from his pocket, draws a short line on the paper. Carefully he tears up first the gray square and then the black square.

"Care to add anything?" asks Hauser.

"You're guessing," says Gahern.

"Am I?" asks Hauser, and standing up leaves Gahern alone in the room. He leaves behind the scraps of squares, the pencil, the paper.

Outside, he takes a place looking through the mirrored wall. Next to him are four people whom he chooses to represent in the following fashion: oval, triangle, rhombus, triangle. Through the mirrored wall, he watches Gahern sit at the table, head in his hands. He seems, for once, shaken. Hauser goes to fetch a cup of hot water; when he comes back, nothing has changed.

"Now what?" asks one of the shapes beside him.

Oval. Red, Hauser thinks, *perhaps orange*. Hauser holds one hand before his face to assure himself it is still a hand, then shrugs. "Wait," he says. "Nothing to do but wait."

He watches through the glass. Having sipped away his water, he goes in search of another cup.

When he comes back he finds Gahern has pulled his chair about to bring his back to the mirrored wall. He has taken up the pencil, is hunched over the paper, his arm moving furiously. Hauser wishes he could see Gahern's face.

Gahern remains hunched over for some time. At last he puts down the pencil, brings both hands together before his body to do something with the paper. Hauser finishes his water, but does not go back for more.

When finished, Gahern pulls his chair back to its usual place at the table. He has folded the sheet of paper into a white box, a simple cube. The pieces of the squares are nowhere to be seen.

Something has happened, thinks Hauser. *Something always does.*

But what?

Once Gahern has been returned to his cell, Hauser enters, sits alone with the box. He examines it, draws a picture of it in his notebook. It is the sort of box that children make, and having made them himself as a child, he knows which seam he must unfold first. He knows what to do.

He turns the seam and the box cracks open. Inside are the scraps of the black and gray squares. Dumping them out onto the tabletop, he forms a little heap. He unfolds the next seam, then the next, until the box lies flat on the table, nothing but a creased piece of paper.

There is nothing written on the paper. Indeed, all that remains of Hauser's original mark is a thinness in the paper where
Gahern has fastidiously rubbed said mark away.

An hour later, Hauser is still staring at the blank sheet of
paper, at the pile of scraps. Perhaps it is a denial, perhaps a
confession, but in either case, he is no closer to understanding
anything. There is no point, he knows from past experience, in
asking Gahern to explain further.

He looks at his watch. He begins to piece the squares back
together, the black one representing, he can still bother himself
to recall fleetingly, the wife, the gray one representing her new
husband.

Soon the investigation will be taken from him. He will pass
along the evidence—the fragments of squares, the folded sheet
of paper—and then he will tender his resignation to a dirty white
oval. Leaving Branner B for good, leaving the unrepresented
Gahern, he will walk into the street and lose himself in the crowd
among shapes of all kinds. Until then, there is nothing to do but
wait.

The Ex-Father

And then, as if suddenly, their mother was dead by her own hand, the two young girls inherited by the ex-husband, their father, the ex-father. The ex-father moved back from his solitary apartment across the country with two small suitcases of clothes, a carload of books, and a large boxful of ball-and-socket joints and rods and latex molded into doll parts. At first he did not allow them to touch the doll parts, kept them from them until he had dumped all the latex into the tub and warmed pans of water on the stove to pour over them. Only then did he show them where each piece was designed to go, how the latex fit around the rods and joints, how to connect each ball to each socket, but when they had finished, all they had were four feet and two legs and two hips, the lower halves of two girls, of two dolls, two sets of half-girls. Nearly the same size as half of the girls themselves, but with nothing but air higher up.

"Is that all?" asked the youngest.

"Yes," said the ex-father, looking nervous, "that's all."

"What happened to the rest?" the oldest girl asked. But the ex-father just looked confused and in need of help, as if with such a question she had taken him past the limit of his parenting expertise. The oldest girl didn't understand what she had said wrong. The oldest girl wondered if maybe he would call someone in to explain to them whatever he felt needed to be explained, just as after their mother had died by her own hand the Church had sent someone wearing a button-up sweater to try to make things clear to them.

Their mother had *passed on*, the churchman had told them. She had gone to a better place, was living a better life. They were not to blame for what had happened. The oldest girl had never considered the possibility that they might be to blame for what had happened, but the churchman was so insistent that it was not their fault that she began to believe that yes, probably somehow it was their fault. The youngest girl felt the same, or something at least, for she started to cry, and it was up to the oldest girl to comfort her. It had always been up to the oldest girl to comfort her, ever since the father had left to become the ex-father.

Just because she had died by her own hand, the churchman admitted just before taking them off to let them stay with another family until their ex-father could move back in, did not necessarily mean she wouldn't go to heaven. It was a talk that might have worked too, and mostly did for the youngest girl, despite her crying, but it would not work for the oldest girl for the simple reason that of the two girls the oldest had been the only one to see the mother dead. Nobody knew this about her. Nobody knew that the oldest girl knew that *by her own hand* did not mean pills or exhaust fumes or anything like that, but that while they were at school the mother had taken a serrated knife and tried to hack her own head off with it. She had not managed to cut the head all the way off but had gotten pretty far, and the oldest girl had gone to Church herself for enough years to know that nobody who wanted to cut their head off as bad as that was going anywhere near heaven. Because of what she had seen she was more grown-up than the churchman, she knew, and than her ex-father too, and if she hadn't had her sister to comfort she would have told the churchman enough of what she had seen so he could know to speak to her in a different voice and use the words he was hiding from now.

But there had been her sister to protect, as had been the case earlier as well when the police had squatted beside her and asked her what of her mother she'd seen. But she didn't want them to take her away from her sister, so she said, *Nothing*. Then how had she known that her mother was dead? She didn't know, she claimed. She had come into the house and called out and nobody had answered and there was a weird smell so she had left. But how was it that she had sent her sister to the neighbor's house quite some time before going over herself? *I thought at first my mother wasn't home*, she lied, *but that there was something wrong in the house, so I decided to stay in the yard and wait for her to come*. And the policemen, who must have known she was lying, were not grown-up enough to want to know what had really happened, and had allowed that to stand.

In fact, what she had done was open the door and smelled something, but not thought twice, and she and the youngest girl had dumped their backpacks onto the couch and went into the kitchen to have some bread. The way they liked their bread was squished; they liked to take a piece of it and crush it down in their fists until it was a dense ball, and then sit on the counter and nibble away at it, sometimes pretending to be animals; mice usually, but other animals too. That was the way the ex-father, when he had been the father, had liked to eat bread in the afternoon, and that was how they liked to do it too. In the middle of doing it, the oldest girl had put the ball of bread on the counter and on the way to the bathroom had met the cat and then petted it and only then realized that it was leaving tracks of blood along the wooden floor. At first she thought the cat's paws were hurt, but no, the paws were fine, and then she had followed the tracks back to her mother's bedroom to find her mother inside, lying on the floor dead after trying to saw off her own head. Part of her couldn't stand to look but the rest of her could only think that this was something the sister must not see, that she, the oldest girl, must stay calm, must protect the sister. So she went out and finished her breadball and then coaxed the sister down to the neighbor's house and then came back on her own. She went into the backyard and tried to dig a hole in the garden for the mother, like they had done once for the cat, but the hole took too long to dig and her mother was too big, so, still calm, she stopped digging and then stayed in the backyard alone awhile, looking at the little hole, still calm, and then went over to the neighbor's house herself and very carefully called the police.

So, in place of the mother, they now had the ex-father and the two half-dolls. The ex-father did not know that he was called the ex-father. He was called that because the mother had some-times called him that, as if in moving out of the house he was no longer their father. It was true that after he had moved out, they no longer saw him much anymore. He had called them once a week, from his tiny apartment across the country, and every week he asked them the same questions. The oldest girl did not understand why he asked the same questions every time and wondered if he had a list he was looking at or if it was just that he thought the answers to the same questions should be chang-ing quicker than they did. The youngest girl always answered the questions and seemed happy, but the oldest girl had found it difficult to think of anything to say at all. Sometimes, because of that, the ex-father would ask the same question over again, as if whatever response she had first managed to give was wrong and needed to be corrected before their relationship could go on.

Now the ex-father was back in the town, back in the house, making at least something of an effort to be the father rather than the ex-father. But he was not good at it anymore, at being the father. Like on the telephone, he asked the same questions over and did not always seem to understand when a question had been answered. The youngest girl would sit on his lap and hug him and that seemed to make him less afraid of her, but the oldest girl felt too old for that and did not know what else to do. So, she was polite to the ex-father. She listened to his questions and answered them and was polite, but despite this he still seemed a little afraid of her—or maybe because of it. But what else, the oldest girl wondered, was there for her to do?

Since the mother's death by her own hand, the youngest girl had been sleeping with the older girl in the latter's room. The youngest girl had never liked to sleep alone and often had crept into the mother's room to sleep, waiting until the mother was tired enough or asleep enough not to send her back. When the ex-father was still the father, he had not allowed it, had himself taken the youngest girl back to her own bed each time, at first patiently and then more and more sternly until, to keep the youngest girl from leaving the bed, he had to shout at her. The oldest girl wondered sometimes how it must be for the youngest, alone in the dark and awake and hardly able to stand being alone, but she could not understand it herself. The oldest girl had never minded sleeping alone, had never crept in to sleep with the mother. If she had difficulty in sleeping it was because there was another body in the bed beside her, the body of her sister. Or, better put, simply her sister, for the word body made her think of other things now. She, the oldest girl, had difficulty going into parts of the house, into her mother's room, and if she went in at all it was only so as not to reveal to the sister that she was afraid. The sister, though, had been successfully protected: she could go into the mother's room and stay in there and think nothing of it. Even the ex-father had, almost without thought, immediately moved into the mother's room, the room that when he had been the father used to belong to him as well. He slept there and didn't seem to think twice about it. And he said nothing either about the youngest girl sleeping in the oldest girl's room. Things that had not been allowed when he was the father were allowed now that he was the ex-father. He was in the house, pretending to be part of the family, when in fact he was more like a ghost.

After school, the two girls played together. Sometimes they played with the doll-parts, the ex-father watching nervously on as they assembled and disassembled the two half-dolls, walked them about. At times, late at night, the oldest girl thought she

could hear the ex-father dumping boiling water over the parts
again in the bathroom, but perhaps he was doing something
else. In any case, every morning the dolls had been taken apart
again and were back in the box. After school, the girls reas-
sembled the half-girls and walked them about the house, dressed
them in their own pants and shoes and panties, set them up with
their legs crossed on the couch.

That lasted for a while. When they got bored of it, they
figured out that any ball could connect to any socket and they
made a single odd girl, a whirl of legs, her bottom half legs, her
top half legs, and set her up in corners to see how she would
look. She was like a spider, somehow, the doubled half-girl, and
it disturbed the ex-father enough that once they had made the
doubled half-girl he would always leave the room and go into
the kitchen and pour a drink. In the old days, when he had been
the father, he had not been allowed to drink in front of the girls,
the mother had not allowed it. Both girls had been a little younger
but they had known the father drank even when they were young.
Once, even, the oldest girl had asked him about it and he had
said, *Do you really want to know? Because I'll tell you if you really want to know,* and the oldest girl decided no, from the way
he was saying it there was something wrong with talking about
it, and she knew anyway after all, so there was no point. Even
now he drank not exactly secretly, but furtively. He went into
the kitchen and poured a drink and then drank it there, standing
at the sink, washing out his glass afterward. But if the oldest girl
came in the ex-father would gamely turn to face her and not try
to hide the drink, would even hold the drink where she would
have to see it, so not hidden exactly, but what exactly she could
not say. And in any case you could always tell by the smell of his
body, the way his sweat smelled. And now at night when he
came to kiss them his breath didn't smell like his breath, and she
had this year stopped kissing him, would instead just hug him,
listen to his heavy voice, feel his warm, wet breath on her neck.

There had been some protest, when the decision had been
made that the ex-father would return to the house and live in it

as he had back when he had been the father, some protest from
the mother's mother. The mother's mother claimed the ex-father
was not a fit parent, that he was wrong for the two girls, that he
would not raise them in proper fashion. By this the mother's
mother meant that the ex-father would not raise them in the
Church that he had left upon leaving the house and divorcing
the mother. But religion, apparently, so the oldest girl gathered,
was not a matter the court considered important, or at least not
sufficiently important to deprive the children of their ex-father.
In the suicide note the mother wrote, she had stated that the
only reason she had not taken the girls "with her to God" was
because they were too young for her to bear taking their lives by
her own hand. She was weak, just as she had been weak, she
claimed in the note, in letting the father leave the Church and
abandon all of them. She was a weak woman, the mother claimed.
But the oldest girl could not think of the mother as a weak
woman, having seen the way in which she had managed to
nearly saw her head off. The oldest girl had no memory of reading the suicide note in the mother's bedroom, she was so busy
concentrating on keeping calm and protecting her sister, but she
must have read it, for though nobody had said anything to her
about it she could see the letter and all the words on it written
out by her mother in her own hand. Sometimes she thought she
had imagined the letter, but she had overheard the ex-father say
just enough about it in a roundabout way on the telephone to
know she had not imagined it, that she remembered it perfectly.
Another portion of the letter had been what she had come to
think of as the bequeath portion. In it, her mother had written
that she *bequeathed her children to their grandmother.* "Bequeath," the oldest girl had overheard the ex-father say into the
phone one day after he had stood at the sink long enough to
rinse out his glass four times. "Bequeath, bequeath. Can you
imagine? As if they're chattle or something." The oldest girl was
not certain what either bequeath or chattle meant, but she did
know from another overheard telephone conversation that the
bequeathing hadn't worked, that it was something you could do
with property but not with people, and the fact that the mother

had tried to do it was an indication of how much, according to the ex-father, she had been *brainwashed by God*. The oldest girl liked it when the ex-father talked like this; it was more like the father. But it never lasted long. Whenever he thought she might be listening he became a ghost again, without opinions, an ex-father.

There must be a way, the older girl often thought, to snap the ex-father back into being the father again, but she was not sure how to go about it. There are words that work, she knew, like when the churchmen had shown up at the door with a casserole and tried to get in the house, and the ex-father kept trying to get them to leave but nothing he could say would do it, and finally she had heard the ex-father become the father and use the word *goddamn*, and that single word, unless it was two words, had driven them off the porch at last. But when the father had turned and saw her, and realized that she had heard, he quickly reverted to being the ex-father again.

It was a word she knew about but that she had never heard said inside the house before. It did something to her as well as to the churchmen, but she made the choice not to turn away. *Goddamn*, she made the inside of her head say. Maybe that word would work on the ex-father too, drive him away and bring the father back.

There were moments of that sort, brief sparks, where the ex-father threatened to become the father again, but as time went on the older girl realized that they, both girls, were in danger of losing the father altogether, and perhaps not only the father but the ex-father as well. Often when they came home from school, the ex-father would not be in the house. That moment of going into the house and calling out and getting no response always took the oldest girl back to the day she had found her mother dead, and she had to force her feet to move into the house. She would not have been able to do it if it hadn't been for the youngest girl, the need to protect her, the need to pretend everything was all right. But, she wondered, where is the person that is supposed to protect me? But the oldest girl steeled herself and did it, and as time went on she had to do it more and more. Sometimes the ex-father would leave a note but sometimes not even that. He would leave bowls of macaroni in the fridge for them to eat and he would either come back just as they were going to bed or sometimes they would find him in the morning, his shirt half off, lying on the floor. He would get up and wander about looking harried and guilty as they got ready to leave for school, a bad smell to his skin, and when they were going out the door he was already standing beside the sink. Sometimes the oldest girl would wake up in the middle of the night to hear him blundering about, knocking everything over, only sometimes she was still asleep and imagined it was the mother knocking into walls as she sawed off her own head. It was more weight on the oldest girl and more to do, and sometimes she felt like she was the only grown-up. She woke in the middle of the night to go to the bathroom, but found the father there, naked and asleep in the cold water of the tub. To use a bathroom, she had to go down the hall and through the mother's dark room and into the bathroom there, and after that, after being in the mother's room in the dark, she couldn't go back to sleep. She lay in bed wondering what, if anything, she could do to make the ex-father understand, what word she could use. But there was nothing, no word, that was a sure bet. *Goddamn*, she thought. She lay in the dark until it began to get light outside and then she stayed watching her sister sleeping beside her, the blanket pushed down to the bottom of her ribs, and then suddenly the oldest girl knew:

When the girls came home from school, the ex-father was not there, had left no note. The girls sat on the kitchen counter mashing their bread into balls and nibbling slowly, the youngest girl trying to get the oldest to pretend with her, the oldest ignoring her. The oldest girl just kept chewing her bread, and when she had finished started to mash up another piece. In the end, the youngest girl gave up, finished her bread, and went downstairs to turn on the T.V.

The oldest girl got the boxful of doll parts out and put it in the living room. She stayed looking at it a while and then went

into the kitchen to mix up a pitcher of apple juice, then got out
the food coloring, mixed in color after color until the color cor-
responded, roughly, to what she remembered. She took bread
and tore it into tiny, tiny pieces and put it into the colored juice.

The youngest girl came upstairs just as the oldest girl was
putting one of the half dolls together and was starting on the
next. *It's a game*, the oldest girl told her, *a funny joke*. The youngest girl wanted to help.

Together the girls dressed the half-dolls in their own clothes,
their own pants and shoes and panties. They dumped them
akimbo just outside the bathroom door and then poured the
colored apple juice all about on the floor and on the half-dolls
and on the oldest girl's chest, and hoped it looked like blood,
the sodden bits of bread like clotting. The oldest girl tried to
think of how the mother had looked when she found her and in
the end thought, yes, for a moment anyway, it might do. All I
need, she thought, is just a moment, and the right words.

The youngest girl is jumping around and giggling, waiting
for the joke. The oldest girl does not know what this will do to
her, but, she thinks, she does not know what else to do. She
gives the youngest girl three spoonfuls of cough syrup. Soon,
the youngest girl will be hiding in the bathtub, giggling still, but
with a little luck the ex-father will come home late enough that
the cough syrup will have worked, and the youngest girl will be
asleep. The oldest girl will try to get her up and into bed. And
then the oldest girl will come back and lay again on the floor,
her feet propped on the tub, the door half open so that from the
hall you can see her head and her stained chest but nothing
below, a half-girl. She will hear her ex-father stumbling about
outside, then his key scraping in the lock, and then he will come
in and stop dead, and think her dead, and grow up, and then at
last he will be the father again. And then, before he can turn
back, she will stand up and tell him every goddamn thing and
make everything right for good.

The Intricacies of Post-Shooting Etiquette

I.

One winter morning, watching Bein read his breakfast paper, Kohke decided to kill him. He stood behind Bein, aligned a pistol barrel with Bein's skull and worked the trigger. He had reasons for wanting Bein dead, but watching his lover shake about the floor, smearing blood on the linoleum, he could not bring those reasons to mind.

The pistol must have wavered when he pulled the trigger, for Bein did not seem to be dying properly. After a writhing agony he fell still, attempting to catch his breath. And then, calmly, he asked Kohke to call an ambulance.

Unable to bear the thought of shooting Bein again, Kohke carried the pistol from room to room, finally submerging it in a pitcher of orange juice. He telephoned for help. Paramedics arrived, the police alongside. The first extracted Bein. The second discovered the pistol, remanded Kohke to custody.

In an interiorly-mirrored room, Kohke began to lie. He had not known the gun was loaded. He had pointed it at Bein only as a prank. He had thought it a novelty cigarette lighter, not a real gun. He lied even about matters of no consequence. Slowly the lies accumulated, crowding each other awkwardly. Yet, when the police received word that Bein, rolling into surgery, had absolved Kohke of blame, they grudgingly released him.

In this fashion a measure of uncertainty slipped into Kohke and Bein's relationship. Never having shot anyone close to him before, Kohke had difficulty unraveling post-shooting etiquette. *Was the relation terminated?* Kohke wondered, as he waited for Bein's release. *Could they be said, now, properly, to have a relationship?* Had the shooting freed him of sexual and emotional obligation to Bein? Or had any potential release been countermanded by Bein's refusal to blame him?

What, wondered Kohke, *did Bein actually know?* Officially the shooting was classified as an accident. Perhaps even Bein himself believed it to be an accident: after all, he had not seen Kohke pull the trigger. *Or perhaps*, thought Kohke, *Bein has only classified it such so as to be able, later, to avenge himself against me*.

Alone in the large bed, beset with uncertainty, Kohke had trouble sleeping. He would awaken, the stench of gunpowder strong in his nostrils, feeling he had been shot. The day after the accident he contemplated visiting Bein in the hospital, but he could not bear to see Bein so soon, partly from shame, partly from fear of violating post-shooting etiquette. How does one apologize for shooting someone? *Sorry to have shot you, Bein* didn't ring properly, but neither did *My apologies for the accident, Bein*. On the second day, he stayed away because he could develop no convincing lie to justify his first-day's absence. By the third day, the pattern was fixed. Visiting Bein now would seem unusual.

He kept himself apprised, bribing an intern named Chur to provide him daily reports. It was from Chur he learned of Bein's transfer from critical to stable condition. From Chur, he learned that bullet fragments had lodged in Bein's brain, causing blindness. He was told that the second bullet—

"The second what?" asked Kohke.

"Bullet," said Chur.

"Bullet?"

"Yes, of course," said Chur. "Mr. Kohke, you fired twice."

Second bullet? He had no memory of firing a second bullet. Indeed just the opposite: he remembered shooting once and not again. How had he managed to blot out this second bullet which, according to Chur, had rendered Bein immobile, paralyzed from the neck down?

Presenting himself at the police station, he asked to examine his arrest report. The sergeant assigned to the case chatted at him idly while Kohke thumbed through the file. Yes, he saw, there had been two bullet wounds, one in Bein's skull, the second in his back. Two cartridges were absent from the orange juice-drenched pistol. He had fired twice. His body had pulled the trigger while his mind remained at a safe remove.

Research led him to understand where he had gone wrong. The caliber of the pistol he had found in Bein's top drawer had been woefully inadequate. It was, he learned during an awkward park bench conversation with a war veteran, more appropriate for the slaughter of dogs, small children.

The police had the gun now. Despite his awkward success soliciting the veteran in the park, Kohke could not imagine entering a munitions shop to purchase a more powerful weapon. It went contrary to his character. Nor would the police so easily excuse a second incident.

Perhaps, he thought, *the relationship has been successfully terminated and I will never see Bein again*. Or perhaps when Bein did come home, crippled, he would prove a different man. A so-called *new man*. Then, the circumstances that had culminated in the shooting would not accumulate again. Yet even in the best of circumstances, Kohke was not certain he could bear living with a man he himself had crippled.

In the midst of such reflections, the hospital telephoned. Bein would be released in four days. He had requested that Mr. Kohke take him home. Was Mr. Kohke willing to accept responsibility for Mr. Bein?

No, he said, *all apologies*, and recradled the headpiece.

He sat beside the telephone, scrutinizing the pale lampshade. Apparently the relationship was not terminated after all, but continued to limp on.

It would look suspicious both to Bein and to the police if he refused to take Bein in. He could ill afford suspicion. He had been hasty, foolish.

Holding his hand out to the lampshade, he greeted it enthusiastically. Getting up, he went to look at himself in the mirror. In the glass he could still perceive the old, pre-shooting Kohke, largely intact. *Hail, fellow*, he thought.

"Bein," he said to the mirror. "What a pleasure to see you again."

Watching his face as he said it, he saw no revelation of anything, let alone guilt. Surely Bein, blinded, would notice less than he. He closed his eyes.

"How was your stay?" he heard his voice smoothly say. "I must apologize for not visiting. I had been informed that healing takes place more rapidly in solitude."

I will keep him off balance, he told himself. *I will give nothing away. I will maintain the upper hand.*

II.

He could not imagine rolling Bein's wheelchair over and over the spot where Bein had been shot. Yet he was concerned that moving would excite his suspicions, allowing Bein to gain the upper hand. Compromising, he rented a new apartment in the same building—one floor lower than the original apartment but identical in every other respect: three dusty rooms, doors sufficiently wide to admit Bein's wheelchair, the final room with a window opening on an airshaft.

At the appointed day's appointed hour, he walked to the hospital. Bein was slumped in the circular drive in his wheelchair, a nurse posted beside him. *You're Mr. Kohke?* she asked as he approached. He nodded. *Kohke?* said Bein.

Kohke nodded again. "Hello, Bein."

"What's wrong?" asked Bein, face squinching.

"Not a thing," said Kohke.

"I don't want to go home with him," Bein said to the circular drive.

"Nonsense," said the nurse.

"I didn't think you'd come," said Bein. "Why did you?"

"I'll leave you two alone now," said the nurse, smiling grimly, then slipping away.

"Well, shall we set off?" asked Kohke, briskly jabbing the wheelchair apartmentward.

They traveled several rugged blocks without speaking. As they passed other people, Bein would turn his head, directing one ear or the other toward their voices. *His ear is his eye*, thought Kohke, listening to the faint clack of the wheels.

"What's wrong?" Bein asked again.

"Nothing," said Kohke.

"Why do you do this?"

"Do what?"

"Refuse to share your feelings with me."

"Bein," said Kohke. "I beg you."

When Bein wouldn't stop speaking, Kohke set the brakes on the wheelchair and abandoned him. He crossed the street and looked at Bein from the other side, watching the foot traffic flow around his lover. He could hear the sound of Bein's voice, see his lips move, but could make out none of what the voice was saying. He stayed, waiting for the moment when Bein would realize he was no longer present.

Was there a way to end the relationship immediately? Could he abandon Bein on the corner?

He stood watching Bein's mouth move until he could not
bear it, then watched instead Bein's wheelchair, and finally turned
to watch the traffic light as it turned, then turned, then turned
again.

When he looked away from the traffic light, it was growing
dark. Bein was just as Kohke had left him, still slumped in his
chair.

"You came back," said Bein, as Kohke affixed his hands to
the grips. Kohke employed a bright voice to respond, the same
voice he employed with dogs and small children: "Of course I
came back." Reaching down, he levered the brakes off, began to
rotate the chair about.

"We're going back?" asked Bein, pale eyes staring not at
Kohke but above him, at Kohke's nonexistent hat.

"Back?"

"To the hospital."

"You've been released, Bein. You can't go back."

"Where am I to go?"

Kohke did not answer. He began to push his lover down the
sidewalk, clicking over cracks until they reached the apartment
building. Holding tight to the chair's vulcanized grips, he took
Bein up the steps backwards, drawing the chair up a tread at a
time, shaking him, regressing a few treads, turning the wheelchair about until he was convinced Bein would be unsure of
how many flights they had mounted. Then he was at the door
and had opened the door and they were both in.

"Welcome home," he said. He lifted his ex-lover out of his
chair and into the bed.

"This is my bed?" Bein asked. "It doesn't feel like my bed."

"Nothing feels the same after you've been shot, Bein."

"How would you know?"

"That's just what they say."

"We're not going back to the hospital?"

He could not bear Bein's face up close. Kohke kept casting
his gaze about, finally letting it rest upon the buttons of Bein's
shirt, a string of tiny, bland faces.

"No," said Kohke to the buttons. "You're done with the hospital. You're home now."

Bein turned his head slightly, dimpling the pillow's case. "Take me back."

Kohke left the room, went to the kitchen. He was thirsty. The refrigerator was unplugged. When he opened it he found that the air inside had turned. He plugged the refrigerator in, closed it.

He listened to the hum of the refrigerator. He could hear Bein's voice abuzz in the bedroom, still speaking. He could not hear what he was saying. He went back, stood with crossed arms in Bein's doorway.

Bein fell silent, whorling one of his ears toward Kohke. He stayed like that, motionless, regarding him with his ear, as Kohke grew uncomfortable.

"What is it?"

"It doesn't feel right," said Bein.

"Don't be crazy," Kohke said.

"What's changed?"

"Nothing. It's all the same."

"It doesn't feel the same."

Kohke went back into the kitchen. He wandered all around the kitchen and then left the apartment. There was the hall, the floorboards brightly polished and throwing light up against his shoes. There was the light switch, apparently innocuous, the paint worn thin upon it. He went back into the kitchen, looked at the refrigerator until he couldn't stand to look any longer. Thirsty, he opened it, found it empty.

He went back to Bein's room. Standing in the doorway, he watched him. Slowly, Bein smiled.

"The sea," said Bein. "I no longer hear the sea."

The sea, thought Kohke later, sitting in the hall just outside the apartment, *What sea?* There was no sea. They were hundreds of miles from the ocean, there was no river or other water within sight or hearing of the apartment. The bullets had damaged Bein's thinking as well as his vision.

"The sea?" he had repeated, standing before Bein.

"Yes," said Bein. "I don't hear it."

"I don't recall having heard a sea," Kohke carefully stated.

"You wouldn't," said Bein.

"What is that supposed to mean?"

"Is the window open?" asked Bein. "Open the window and you'll hear it."

Kohke looked back at the window leading into the airshaft. "I have to go to work," said Kohke. "I can't bother with that now."

"Work?" asked Bein. "You, work?"

"I've changed, Bein," lied Kohke, "I really have. I'm a new Kohke."

Bein contorted his face in a fashion the meaning of which Kohke found difficult to determine. Backing his way to the front door, he left.

On a park bench, ogled by a veteran whose hands fumbled deep within his pockets, Kohke considered life with Bein. Bein had come home with him, which Kohke reluctantly classified as *promising*. Bein had mentioned nothing about the murder attempt, had not blamed him. Also *promising*—unless Bein's silence was seen as *biding his time so as to exact his revenge*. Yet how, he asked himself, could a paralyzed man take revenge? *Disappointing*, though not yet *cause for alarm*, Bein sensed the wrongness of the apartment, felt despite the identical floorplan that he was not at home. Such wrongness, Kohke suspected, could lead to recognition of other wrongnesses, and must be corrected.

Yet the sea? What was this talk of the sea? How could it be classified?

Deserting the bench he returned to the apartment building, borrowed the key for his former apartment from the manager. He went from room to room, listening, first with windows closed, then with windows open, then some opened, some closed. He turned on the water, listened to the pipes tick. He was unable to identify any sound that even remotely recalled the sea. He stood on his toes, squatted down. There was, he saw when crouched, a faint rust of Bein's blood still marring the pebbling of the linoleum. Hurriedly, he left.

Bein's brain must have fused two memories, dredging a past sea into his present life, or simply evoking water from empty air. *The sea*, he told himself, returning the key between thumb and forefinger to the manager. *He wants the sea. The sea is what he'll have.*

III.

He purchased a tape recorder and a cassette series entitled *The Soothing Power of Nature*. In the back room, he opened the window, plugged the recorder in, set it on the sill. The cellophane crackled stiffly coming off *The Soothing Power of Nature*. He dropped the cassettes into the airshaft, except for one, marked *Aqua Vitae*, which he inserted into the machine.

When he pressed play, he heard a short feed of blank tape, then the sound of waves. He listened for a time, set the recorder to play continuously.

Bein was lying on the bed, his head sunk deep into the pillow, his blind eyes wandering the upper rim of his orbits.

"Good morning," said Kohke. "How are we today?"

"Give me to someone else," said Bein.

"We don't know what we're saying this morning," said Kohke, his voice cheery. "Do we?"

"One of us doesn't," said Bein.

Kohke positioned the wheelchair next to the bed, tugged Bein over until he was beside it. He forced Bein's feet onto the floor. Slipping his arms around Bein's chest, he locked them behind his back. He heaved Bein up, dropped him into the chair.

"No need getting dressed today," Kohke said. "We won't go out."

Wheeling Bein to the table, he began to feed him. Bein chewed, then sat awaiting the next bite, mouth ajar. Kohke poured him a glass of orange juice, expecting to see the pistol's snub as the juice in the pitcher drained away. He clacked the glass's rim against Bein's teeth.

"I hear it now," said Kohke as Bein swallowed.

"Hear what?"

"The sea," he said. "I hear the sea."

"Sea?" said Bein. "What do you mean?" And, once Kohke wheeled him back, pushed him back into the bed: "You're hearing things, Kohke. Imagine that."

The cassette ran nearly constantly. Despite Kohke's efforts at preservation, it acquired a dull hiss, degenerated into a sound hardly recognizable as water. It had been a mistake to buy the tape, to try to simulate something that hadn't existed in the first place. Yet, now that it was done, Kohke felt he had committed himself.

Oddly, as the tape deteriorated Bein perked up, claimed to recognize what he heard as waves. Kohke could not tell if Bein was toying with him or if, somehow, he heard it now. Perhaps it was simply whatever dementia that had first caused Bein to believe the sea existed had now returned. It had all gone wrong, Kohke felt, and there was no putting things right. Better to let the tape run down to its own extinction.

This was how Kohke came to identify the waning of his relationship with Bein. When the tape snapped, the relation would end and he would be free of Bein. He wasn't certain how this end would occur, but he was certain it would.

Bein began begging Kohke to take him down to the sea. He wanted to touch the water's edge.

"You wouldn't feel it," said Kohke. "No point."

No, insisted Bein, his face would feel it. He wanted Kohke to carry him down to feel the breeze, then out into the water in his arms. They would walk out until Bein's face was floating, licked by the waves.

"Like a lily," Bein said.

I can't stand it, thought Kohke.

He was tied to Bein, obligated to him until the tape broke. Still, there were distractions. There was the veteran in the park with his fluid and somewhat inarticulate consolations. It was better than nothing, though all the while he thought of Bein alone in the apartment, the tape winding slowly down. There was shopping, his imaginary job, other excuses. Yet each time he went back he found the situation less bearable.

He considered simply leaving, abandoning Bein, letting him starve to death, though he worried the neighbors would hear Bein's cries and rescue him. When he had nearly worked up sufficient nerve to desert Bein, the hospital called, inquired after Bein's condition. How was Mr. Bein recovering? Was there anything they could do? They would call again, the intern said. It made Kohke feel he was under observation. *A courtesy call,* the hospital called it. *Courtesy to whom?* wondered Kohke.

Bein refused to eat, clamping his jaw tight enough that Kohke had great difficulty prying his mouth open. At all other times, Bein spoke constantly, sometimes all through the night, with little order or logic, Kohke trying to find a hidden sense in what he was saying. The stench of Bein seeped into the floors, Bein's skin beneath his clothing starting to weep after Kohke began to neglect cleaning him. There was the veteran in the park, then the return home, then Bein's voice again asking for Kohke to carry him down to float in the water.

"Like a lily," Bein said again. "A water lily."

"Too steep," said Kohke, gritting his teeth. "Too rocky. Too dangerous."

Bein kept asking. He was willing to take the risk, Bein said, and if Kohke was to lose his balance and fall, Bein would absolve him of all blame. "Write a statement absolving yourself of blame," he said to Kohke. "Put a pen in my mouth and I'll sign it."

As the tape became sheer hiss and squeal, Bein became more insistent. He must go to the sea, Kohke must take him. He spoke about it, talked it through, until Kohke covered his ears. He sat in place, watching Bein in bed, listening to the rumble of Bein's voice gone inarticulate through his hands. Yet, no matter how silently he covered his ears, Bein would stop talking.

"You've stopped listening," he would say, then lapse into brooding silence. Yet as soon as Kohke uncovered his ears, Bein would begin speaking again.

It made Kohke wonder if Bein could see, if he had regained his sight after all.

Kohke grew nervous, distraught. Bein, however, seemed calmer and calmer, focused on the sea.

"If we can't climb all the way down, at least get me closer," Bein suggested.

"Close? You want close?" Kohke knew his voice was too loud, strident, but could do nothing to tame it. He gathered Bein in his arms, strapping him into the wheelchair, rolling him quickly from his bedroom through the hall and to the back room. There, near the wall, near the window, he reached out and turned the volume up.

"You want closer?" he said. "This is closer."

He watched Bein sit, head cocked, just a few paces from the tape recorder, listening, smiling. The tape speeded and slowed as it played. Kohke watched the awful smile, Bein's face all aglow. At first Kohke only watched, without comfort, and then, disturbed, he approached, ready to push Bein out the window.

Yet, as he came close, Bein turned his head and seemed to look right at him. The smile on his face tightened. Kohke stopped. Even when, a few moments later, Bein's eyes drifted in opposite directions, Kohke found he could not bring himself to push Bein out.

He would be a new man, he told himself. When the tape broke, etiquette would be satisfied and he would end the relationship. *Bein, we're not right for each other—you prefer the ocean and I prefer the mountains.* Or, *I want to give you the opportunity to see other people, Bein.* Someday, he told himself, Bein would thank him. He could last until the tape broke if he could get Bein to stop talking about the sea. He would last that long, then he would bathe Bein, feed him, and get rid of him.

Perhaps, Bein suggested, Kohke could construct some sort of sling and lower Bein down until he was safe at water's edge. Certainly that could be done.

Kohke did not respond.

Or if not a sling perhaps Kohke could navigate the path to the water alone until he felt more confident. Then with sheets he could construct a kind of harness and strap Bein to his back. Or perhaps he could fill a backpack with rocks to simulate Bein's weight. Eventually, argued Bein, Kohke would have the confidence and skill needed to carry him flawlessly down to water's edge.

Kohke chose not to respond.

Or there was a way to wrap Bein up, Bein suggested, so that only his face was uncovered, to muffle and swaddle him in blankets so that if he was dropped the injuries would be minimal or at least nonfatal.

"Be quiet, Bein."

"Even if I broke a limb," said Bein, "I wouldn't feel it. It seems to me a worthy risk."

Face quivering, Kohke left the room. He went into the back room, looked at the tape recorder. He walked back past Bein's room, Bein still talking, and into the kitchen, staring first at the hot plate, then the refrigerator.

He went out into the hall, down to the bottom of the steps, then climbed back to the apartment, shutting the door softly behind him. He listened. Bein was no longer speaking.

He crept forward to stand in Bein's doorway, looked in. Bein's head was moving slightly on the pillow, the pillow moving as well. The pillow and head taken together seemed a living creature. The remainder of his body seemed a separate object, part of the bed.

"Or how about this?" started Bein.

"Please," said Kohke, covering his ears, "not another word."

IV.

Sitting in the park, he began idly to gather smooth stones, filling his pockets with them. Later, in the apartment with Bein, he took them out, washing them in the kitchen sink, then placed them in the bathroom, on the counter, the floor. He brought in a fan to give the illusion of a breeze.

Later, he carried a fist-sized stone into Bein's room, brushed it against Bein's cheek. Bein's head jerked.

"What's this?" he asked.

"Stone," said Kohke. "From the sea. The beach rather."

"The sea?" he said, as if the memory of water had ebbed away and left him.

The stone fit Kohke's hand well. It would be easy to lift it up, then bring it down hard. Would Bein's head crack with a single blow? No. Even two bullets had not been enough. How could a stone do better?

"Shall we go to the sea?" Kohke asked.

Bein seemed nervous. "I don't want to go," he said.

"You've begged me for days."

"Something is wrong."

"It's too late," said Kohke. "You're going."

He went into the kitchen, removed the cardboard canister of salt from the shelves, carried it into the bathroom. *When it rains, it pours*, he thought. He opened the faucets, set the plug.

He dumped the entire canister into the bath. The salt swirled in, gathering as a pale silt at tub's bottom, slowly dissolving.

He went to the back room. Unplugging the tape recorder, he carried it into the bathroom, plugged it in again, the tape giving off now a mere shadow of recognizable sound. He went after Bein.

"Come on," he said.

"I don't want to go," said Bein.

"You don't know what you want anymore."

He rolled Bein to the edge of the bed. He left him, turned off the bathwater.

With twine, he knotted Bein's hands together. Pulling Bein off the bed, he stood him up, forced his own head through the space between Bein's arms. With Bein slung like a cape on his back, he began dragging him about.

He jumped up and down a little, scraped Bein along walls, climbed up and down chairs. He pretended to stumble, pressed hands against knees, breathed hard.

"I told you it was a tough climb," he said.

Slowly he threaded his way to the bathroom. Untying Bein's wrists, he sat him against the side of the tub, careful not to let his head touch anything but air.

"We're here," said Kohke.

"We're here?"

Dragging Bein up and over the lip of the tub, he slowly eased him in.

"Here's your sea," said Kohke. "Enjoy."

He had to bend Bein's knees to get him in properly while keeping his head shy of the rim of the tub. He lowered the head down to touch water. Supporting the back of the neck, he lowered it further, until water filled the ears and lapped near the edges of the mouth. There was an expression of confusion to the face and then, slowly, the same disconcerting smile.

"You're holding me," said Bein.

"Yes," said Kohke.

"Let me go," Bein said. "Just for a moment."

Kohke waited until Bein drew a breath, then slipped his hand out from beneath the neck. Bein lay idle in the water, chest tight, head afloat, legs crammed against the spigot.

"I can float," Bein said between breaths. "See?"

"I can see," said Kohke. He picked up a stone from the floor, moving it idly from one hand to the other.

"It's just my head," said Bein. "No body anymore." He smiled broadly. "You've reduced your lover to nothing more than a head, Kohke."

Was it an accusation? It was unbearable, this life with Bein, a sort of existence between life and death. He was miserable. But then, as he thought, he came to feel that before that, even when Bein was whole, he had been miserable as well. Why else would he have shot Bein? And before that, before he had met Bein, he had been miserable as well. Why else would he have searched out Bein at all? Whether Bein knew or not, whether he was in jail or free, alive or dead, Kohke's life would continue in misery. He would continue, yet Bein, only a head who recognized himself as only a head, was content to float in an artificial sea. *He has sucked my life away and taken it for his own*, thought Kohke. Yet, even as he thought it, Kohke knew Bein had taken nothing from him, that he, Kohke, was merely looking for an excuse to end the relationship before the tape snapped.

He took the rock he had been fumbling from hand to hand and placed it on Bein's chest.

Bein started to slip lower into the water. He tipped his head back, his eyes filling with water, his chin jutting up like an iceberg's tip. Kohke added a second stone. Some water trickled into Bein's mouth. "All right," said Bein. "Hold me again."

Putting another stone in place, Kohke said nothing. He watched as Bein tried to expand his lungs, keep above water.

"Kohke?" said Bein, gargling. "Grr-ogrr-eehh?"

As he watched, Bein struggled for breath, breathing in and coughing up great gouts of water. Kohke's body too felt heavy and immobile, as if it were helpless. The head shook and turned under the surface, its hair floating and swaying, bubbles spilling from its nose. The head struggled. The body remained calm and motionless, an obscene and swollen ballast. The head kept trying to breathe, the water roiling above its face as it sucked more water in.

The lips parted and tried to speak but Kohke could make out none of the words. There was only the incomprehensible shivering of lips. Then the head too stopped moving.

The tape was mere static, all water wrung from it. Kohke stayed where he was on the lip of the bathtub. Staring into the water, he awaited the relationship's end.

Promisekeepers

Verl and Laverl and Ray Junior and I are busy pursuing what the literature calls *a special relationship with a few other men.* We are all of us making promises. They are promises this time that we intend to keep, and now that we have a community of brothers to help us, by God we will do it.

The literature, which Laverl's son Xeroxed for us for free on his company machine, says that we have to grant our brothers *asking rights.* They can ask us about God and family, even sex and money. We have discovered that it takes a few beers before honesty kicks in. Beer is not mentioned in the literature we have, so we figure it is okay at least until we lay our hands on the full promisekeeping book. We meet at *Larry's Little Ole Shack* on Highway 51 because it is named after a man and there are no women there to speak of. There is a happy hour from five to seven. We have decided to meet at ten to five not because of the

price of beer but, as Ray Junior says, because it is happy hour
and we are men itching to be happy.

We do not have all the literature because Laverl's son says
he did not have enough time to copy it all. We have enough to
know that we've got our hands on a good thing. Mainly all we
have are the seven promises, but these are crystal clear enough
that we can reason out the rest from there. The literature says we
should *pray with and for one another and to help one another
apply God's Word to our lives.* So while we are waiting for the
clock to inch to five so we can get cut-rate beer, we all bow our
heads. It does not say in the promises we have to pray aloud,
and like hell are we going to in a bar, but I move my lips so that
if any of the others open their eyes they will see me praying in
my heart.

When five strokes on the clock, we open our eyes and call
for beer. We are weary and pierced through by the evils of this
world. Having a beer is like licking your wounds clean so they
can heal. We do not drink to excess but just enough to cleanse
the wounds and to loosen ourselves up to our brothers.

About five beers in, we are open enough to get started.

"I've had a bejesus of a week," says Ray Junior.

We all look at him, serious and open-eared. We all know he
has made, like the rest of us, a promise of *sexual purity*, and that
it is a promise he intends to keep. Ray Junior, by God, is a *man
of integrity*.

"That woman at work again?" asks Verl.

"Hell yes," says Ray Junior. "She don't know when to lay
off."

We shake our heads, watch Ray Junior stare into his beer. He
is the last one we asked to get in on the group. We asked him
because of promise number six, which is that you have to go
beyond *racial and denominational barriers* and meet with a racial man or some sort of heathen once a month. Ray Junior is
both: he is one-sixth Italian (and thus dark-complected) and he is
Episcopalian instead of Southern Baptist. He is going to hell, but
we believe in promise number six so for now he is our brother.

"What did you tell her?" I ask Ray Junior.

"You got to be strong," says Verl.

"I told her I was vowed to sexual purity and I didn't want any more sexual commerce with her."

"I bet that shut her up," I say.

"I bet not," says Laverl.

"You got that one," says Ray Junior, pointing at Laverl. "She kept saying I couldn't just drop her all of a sudden flat. I had to start quoting Scripture at her, using the word of God as a shield and a defense."

We buy him a beer and all slap him on the back and congratulate him for coming through the test. At the same time, we warn him there will be others. Each of us has had tests this week. It is only our promises that have kept us free of harm's way.

Everything keeps on going great and moving forward with our vital relationships with other men. We unburden ourselves and grant one another *the right to inquire*. But then we have a beer or two more and then things start getting a little bit personal. Ray Junior tells us how his finances are a ruin and that he's going to file bankruptcy on his tile business (*Junior Tile*) and gives us the whole beat-up sorry tale of his bad business sense. Verl, he has to tell us that maybe his wife is sleeping around with someone. He gives us all the clues and then wants to know if she is and who it could be. Hell if we know.

"If she's breaking her promises...." he says, and lifts up his thick hand. There is nothing in the seven promises that says we shouldn't give a promise breaker what she deserves.

"What about you?" Ray Junior asks me. "What's wrong with your life?"

"Nothing," I say.

"Nothing?"

"There's got to be something," says Laverl.

"I can't say so," I say. "Things are going pretty well for a change."

"There has to be something," Laverl says again.

"Think," says Verl.

"I'm having a hard time establishing a vital relationship with you if your life is as smooth as all that," says Ray Junior.

"There has to be something."

It is bullshit, but I don't want to get on their bad side. I throw something together on the spot. "My dog has the cancer," I say. "He's not long for this world."

"Your bird dog? Your hunter?"

I nod. "That's the one," I say.

They all start shaking their heads.

"That was a hell of a dog," Ray Junior says, looking weepy, "one hell of a dog. What was its name?"

"Scout," I say.

"Scout," he says. "One hell of a name for one hell of a dog."

"We got to pray for that dog," says Verl. "And for the rest of ourselves too," he says. Before I know it everybody is linked hand-to-hand to his neighbors and right there in *Larry's* Verl is belting out a good old-fashioned out-loud prayer for Scout. It is enough, together with the beer, to make me wish my dog really was sick so we could pray him well.

There comes a slack time where we are getting up one by one to piss and the rest of the time just sitting bland-faced at the table. Happy hour has been gone a while but Verl, I think it is, suggests we go one more round. None of the rest of us sees any reason why we shouldn't.

We are sitting around, drinking again, worn out by the intensity of this *special relationship with other men*, when Laverl gives a little nervous laugh, starts to shake his head.

"What?" asks Verl.

"Nothing," he says.

Then we are back to sitting and staring again, until for no reason Laverl is laughing again and trying to cover his face with one fumbling hand.

"What is it?" asks Verl.

"Yeah," says Ray Junior. "Spill it."

"Oh, Lord," Laverl says. "I just had too much to drink. I sure don't have nothing to say."

"Sure you do," I say.

"We're all brothers here," says Verl. "If you can't tell us, Laverl, you can't tell nobody."

"I'll tell nobody," says Laverl.

"Like hell," says Verl. "Nobody ain't here. Tell us instead. Anything at all, we're your brothers and can help you out."

"We're your brothers," says Ray Junior. "All for Laverl and Laverl for all."

"Out with it, Laverl."

A little more coaxing and finally he puts down his glass and wipes his face. We all cheer. He says, "Remember you asked for it." He puffs out his cheeks and lets the air trickle through slowly.

"It's like this," he says. He picks his glass up and turns it around in his hand. "I don't know how to say it," he says. "So I'll just out and say it. Seems I've taken a fancy to women's underthings."

"What's wrong with that?" says Ray Junior. "We all like to see our women frilled up and half-naked every once in a while."

"Moreso twenty years ago than now," says Verl, and laughs.

"No," says Laverl. "That's not what I mean."

"Well, what do you mean, then?" asks Verl.

"I'm not talking about a woman wearing them."

"You just like looking at them with nobody in them at all?" asks Ray Junior.

Laverl shakes his head.

"What?" says Verl. "What?"

"Don't say it," Ray Junior says. "Shut up."

"I'm talking about me wearing them myself."

"Sweet Jesus," says Verl.

For a while, none of us can really look at Laverl. Verl is looking at his hands. Ray Junior looks at his watch. I take a big drink.

"Jesus, Laverl," says Verl, his voice breaking. "Why'd you have to tell us something like that?"

"I didn't want to tell," he says. "You all made me. Besides, what does it matter? We're still brothers, right?"

"Brothers and sister is more like it," says Verl. "Holy shit."

"What kind of underthings?" I ask.

"Just some of Karen's things."

"Like what?"

"I'm not sure I care to know," says Ray Junior.

"Anything she has around," Laverl says. "Just as long as it's silk. It's the silk I like."

"Hell, they make silk underwear for men," says Verl. "Not that any real man would wear it."

"It's not just the silk," Laverl says. "It's the cut and edging and the whole nine yards."

"I've heard enough," says Verl.

"When do you wear it?" I ask.

"Hell, pretty nearly all the time," Laverl says.

"You mean you're wearing it right now?" asks Verl.

Laverl nods. He unbuttons the top buttons of his wool shirt, quickly opens and closes the gap to flash us a glimpse of a small-cupped bra, the cup folded and stitched down, strapped tight over his hairy chest. Verl gets up with his fist cocked like he's going to punch the hell out of him, then sits down again and looks confused.

"Lard Jesus, I don't even want to know what you have on the bottom," says Verl.

"That can't be Karen's," says Ray Junior. "She's a tad bustier than that. Not that I ever looked."

"It's my daughter's," says Laverl. "I had to extend it in the back.

The rest of us can't help but groan.

"Bartender," says Verl. "I think we better have another round."

Three or four more beers and we start to get our minds around what Laverl has told us. He seems on the surface such a man's man that all this is hard to believe. None of us can understand it. All it says is that it could happen to anyone: you never know when the devil is going to stretch out his finger and touch you right in the head and make you lust after the most unnatural crap in the world. You've got to be every minute of your life embracing sweet Jesus, which our PK organization is getting us to do.

"Is there anything in those promises about promising not to wear women's underthings?" asks Verl. "If there's not, there damn well should be."

"That should be the eighth promise," says Ray Junior.

"I shouldn't have said anything," says Laverl.

"It's said now," I say. "Now we got to get past it."

We order another round.

"So," says Ray Junior. "You still like women, right? You're not a homo, are you? Because I can tell you right now I don't believe there is such a thing as a homo and anybody who thinks he's one is just faking."

"I'm just the same as you in that regard," says Laverl. "I like a woman just as much as the next man."

"That's good, Laverl," Verl slurs. "There's at least that. But we got to warn you that you're on the slippery slope."

"I shouldn't have said it," says Laverl again, shaking his head.

Ray Junior is lining the glasses down the table in as straight a course as he can manage, which is none too straight. "Who's up for another round?" he asks.

"Goddamn it, Laverl," says Verl. "It's none of my business, but you gone and made it my business by telling me. Least you can do is wear real men's underwear when you're meeting with your promisekeeping buddies."

"Hear, hear," says Ray Junior.

"Let's vote on it," says Verl. "All who say Laverl has to wear men's underwear when meeting with us, say 'aye.'"

"Aye," says Ray Junior.

"Aye," says Verl. They both look at me. "Aye," I say. Then all three of us stare at Laverl.

"All right," says Laverl. "I guess I can live with that."

Then everybody is clapping everybody else on the back. We are all pleased that in our very first meeting we have managed to get something done. We sit smiling awhile until slowly we go slack from beer and lack of things to say.

"Shuck them off right now," says Verl.

"What?" asks Laverl.

"There's a bathroom here. Just go right in and shuck them off."

"Hell," says Laverl. "I don't even know that I can walk."

Last call comes and goes. We draw swizzle sticks to see who will be the one to drive the rest home, but damn Verl forgets to tear one shorter than the others so at the end we are all holding swizzle sticks the same size and can't figure out what comes next. We are still trying to figure it out when the bartender comes blowing across the floor and hustles us right out.

We make the door in one piece mostly. Ray Junior gets his forehead a little bloody along the way, but he is drunk enough not to feel it. But maybe he's still stunned or something, because he spends about ten minutes getting his goddamn door open, and then trying to get his car to start. Then he passes out.

We try to shake him awake but he isn't having none of it. We are just pushing Ray Junior over across the seat, trying to decide who gets the next try, when the patrol rolls up.

"You boys aren't planning to drive home in that condition, are you?" Officer Dennings asks.

"No sir," we all say at once, except for Ray Junior who doesn't say anything and Verl who says under his breath, "What condition?" He keeps pushing Ray Junior, trying to get him awake.

"Who's the designated driver here?"

"Don't have one," says Verl. "We're walking."

Laverl ducks down behind Ray Junior's car. He comes up a moment later all pale and puke-splattered, then goes down again.

"All right," says Dennings. "Everybody hand over your keys."

"Dennings," bawls Verl. "I've driven like this a hundred times and nothing ever happened to me."

"Seems like you're about due," Dennings says. "Hand them over."

It takes a while for us all to jumble them out but by God if we don't finally manage. Dennings wants us to go get the keys out of Ray Junior's pocket but like hell if Verl or I are going to reach our hands into another man's pocket. We make Laverl do it because after all he is the one wearing women's underwear.

But we all promise never to say a word about it to Ray Junior.
That too is a promise we intend to keep.

"You can pick them up tomorrow," Dennings says. "At the
station."

He looks at us a while, shining his sidelight on first me, then
Verl, then Laverl, then into the car at Ray Junior.

"All right," he says. "Get in."

"We weren't doing anything," bawls Laverl.

"I'm not taking you in," says Dennings. "I'm driving you
home."

It takes us awhile to get Ray Junior up and out of the car and
into the cruiser. I call shotgun while Verl and Laverl cram in
behind the cage with a rolling-headed Ray Junior between. At
some point Verl and Laverl start singing the school fight song
and yelling "Go Cowboys!" When Dennings tells them to be
quiet they ask him where his school spirit has run off to.

"Don't you like the Cowboys?" asks Verl.

"Sure," says Dennings, "But—"

"—you're not acting like you like the Cowboys," says Verl.

"I like them, but—"

"Let's hear it, then," says Verl. "Put your money where your
mouth is."

Verl starts singing again. Dennings asks him if he wants to
go down to the station and sing it for the judge.

"Nope," says Verl. "Not me. No thanks."

Dennings just shakes his head.

We leave Ray Junior passed out on his lawn. We stumble
back into the patrol car and are off again. I somehow slip forward and crack my head against the dashboard and things get
clearer in some ways, less clear in others. The street lights blur
past and the whole car seems like it is suspended in the thick-
ness of the air, and the lights are moving while we ourselves
stand still.

"Who's next?" asks Dennings.

"Me," says Laverl.

"South Nuttal, right?" asks Dennings.

"Sure," says Laverl. "Three Two Four."

"Three Twenty-Four South Women's Underwear!" bawls out Verl.

"What?" says Dennings.

"He's wearing it," says Verl. "This one," he says, pointing at Laverl. "Right here."

"Ssshhh," says Laverl.

"What?"

"It's true," I say. But it comes out sounding like "Strew."

"Arrest him," Verl calls. "He's wearing frills and lace, by God."

"Is this true?" asks Dennings.

"The whole nine yards," says Verl.

"I'm not gay or nothing," says Laverl.

I cannot help it, but the motion of the car is getting to me.

"I think I'm going to be sick," I say.

"This is a joke right?" Dennings asks Laverl.

"Arrest him, officer," says Verl, hitting me on the back of the head. "He can't be sick in here."

"This is a joke, right?" Dennings says again.

Verl and Laverl start chanting the fight song again. I put my head between my knees and start to groan.

I am dragged off the seat and dropped into the gutter. Verl and Laverl are thrown on top of me, the police cruiser a dim blare of red lights growing distant.

"That was uncalled for," says Verl. "After all I've done for the bastard." He gets up off me, pushes away. He ambles sidewards to the curb and sits heavily down. "Got him into the lodge," he says. "I was going to let him in on keeping promises too, but to hell with him now."

"Climb off," I tell Laverl. After a while he does, and before long we are all sitting on the lip of the gutter, maybe not getting much more sober but hardly getting much more drunk either. We are just like that, a few houses down from where Laverl lives, savoring the dregs of our relationship with a few other men.

"Well," says Verl. "Time to get on home."

But suddenly Laverl is in tears and saying how he doesn't want to go home, that his wife don't understand him and won't even give him the pleasures of the marriage bed because of his choice in underclothing. He says she doesn't understand what her role should be and is even working outside the home which is against God's law, that his marriage isn't like a marriage any-more but only some dead, dried-up shell. All he wants to do, he says, is be a protector and a husband to her but how can he do that when she is stepping outside of her God-given role and hardly even following what is called in the literature *Biblical values?*

"There," says Verl, patting him aback the head. "Buck up, buddy." He reaches into his back pocket, pulls out a flask, hands it to Laverl. "This'll help you some," he says.

Laverl drinks, hands the flask along to me. Damn if the evening doesn't start to pick up again.

Which in a nutshell is how we come to find all three of us squirreled inside of Laverl's house, drunk enough not to remem-ber all the details but together mainly able to puzzle out what happened enough to have the story square for the judge the next day.

Which is how we come to be in Laverl's bedroom at three in the morning, the three of us standing around Laverl's wife. She is in bed, the covers pulled up to her chin, while we are busy calling on the spirit and offering her testimonials of her husband and rendering a true picture of him.

"What the hell is going on?" is the first thing she says, or maybe it is "Oh Lord."

"Ma'am," says Verl. He is so polite that if he had a hat he would be holding it bashfully in his hands. "We apologize for waking you, but it's come to be known among us that there're some problems in your marriage."

"Big problems," says Laverl.

"Big problems," says Verl.

"It's hardly even a marriage anymore," says Laverl.

"That's right," I say. "It's a damn mess."

"We thought we could help out," says Verl. "We thought we could offer you some help."

"Laverl," his wife says, her voice even. "Get these men out of here right now."

Laverl looks at her like she's stupid. "Honey lamb," he says, "Sweetie. These men are here to help us."

"We want you to live up to the promise you made when you married this fine specimen of manhood," says Verl. "We want you to get close to Laverl again."

"Take these men out, Laverl," she says. "And you go with them."

"Honey," he says. "These are Godly men. Give them a chance."

"Maybe you're thinking that your husband is wearing women's underwear because he's gay," says Verl. "But it isn't that."

"He's not gay," I say. "No way."

"I'm not," says Laverl.

"He's straight and ready to prove it."

Laverl's wife picks up the telephone, starts dialing.

"He just likes the feel of silk and lace and crap," says Verl. "It's just a sensation thing. Probably a good hypnotist could cure him."

"That's all," says Laverl. "Scout's honor."

"Lord knows I don't like him wearing it either, but that doesn't mean I'm going to give up on him," says Verl, patting Laverl on the back. "He's a good man. You got to try to understand him. You got to do like the Bible says and cleave fast unto him."

"We'll give you some privacy and let the magic happen," I say.

"So long," says Verl. "Keep an ear to what I said," he says, "and call us if you need us again."

We are starting to back away, Laverl already unbuttoning his clothes, silk spilling out everywhere. His wife is speaking rapidly into the telephone. Laverl puts out his arms and tries to embrace her and she starts smacking him in the face with the headpiece. Verl tells me later that up to that point he was thinking, *This is going to work out just fine*. We figure, though, after that, that we better stay until the magic is actually happening, be there to give Laverl a hand if he needs one. Verl starts singing some Barry White tune to get her in the mood. Laverl can mostly handle her all on his own, but sometimes it helps if you've got a brother to hold an arm or a leg. We are stumbling around the room, struggling to catch hold, giving our support to Laverl and his marriage, when the police arrive.

Müller

...the category through which the world manifests itself is the category of hallucination.

—Gottfried Benn

I.

His grandfather kept sounding like he was choking to death. The attending physician had claimed this was natural, an involuntary reflex—in other words, just because Müller's grandfather sounded like he was choking to death, it did not mean he was choking to death. Still, Müller could not resist plunging his fingers down his grandfather's throat, so as to clear it, and each time he did, he felt the teeth.

The bridge was loose, the bands connected to the real teeth easily slipping off. His grandfather remained semi-conscious, moaning. The bridge came free after Müller pried it back and forth a mere twenty minutes, the post screwed into his grandfather's jaw shearing off sharp. He did not let his wife stop him. He never let his wife stop him. *If the bridge is left in*, he told his wife as he pried, *he might aspirate it. In any case, he's not your grandfather. This is none of your concern.*

II.

He sat in the passenger seat, feeling the row of teeth through his pocket: central incisor, lateral incisor, cuspid, bicuspid. His grandfather liked him, he thought, and now he had stolen his teeth. There had always been teeth, he thought. His whole life, nothing but teeth. His wife was saying something, either to him or the road. He had never been able to smile in a way that showed more than the very tips of his top row of teeth—his wife, when she smiled, showed not only the upper teeth but a stretch of gum above. Other teeth: He had braces when he was a teenager but had failed to finish the treatment; now his mouth was painfully unstable, his teeth and jaw slowly shifting back to their untrammeled state. Other teeth: Once while riding his bicycle he had seen a dog's head hit by the fender of a car, its teeth spattering out and scattering down the road. The car, whose license plate he could still remember, never slowed for an instant. Other teeth: the lover his wife did not know he was seeing, her teeth all at angles, the jagged bite of them against his flesh. He felt in his pocket the four teeth—bicuspid, cuspid, lateral incisor, central incisor. A pocket is not where teeth belong, he thought. The mouth is where they belong. Or a glass. There was noise in the car and he looked up to find his wife smiling softly at him, her mouth closed.

III.

In the dark, Müller kept putting his grandfather's four teeth into his own mouth, slipping them between his lip and teeth. He grimaced, imagining what he would look like with his grandfather's teeth in place of his own, his hair thinning, shoulders hunching, body slowly wasting away. His wife lay beside him, becoming his grandmother. Heat radiated off her; she was still alive. How long would he lie beside her? Nervously he kept taking the teeth out and nervously he slipped them back in again.

He got up from bed, found a mirror. The man in it was hardly familiar, his mouth oddly bunched, neither himself nor his grandfather. He did not know what such as man was capable of. Müller went and found some pliers. He opened the jaws of the pliers, opened his own jaws as well, carefully clamped the pliers around a central incisor. He had to open his jaw wider than was comfortable, and still one of the pliers' grips was wedged against his lower lip. The rasp of the scored metal against his tooth's enamel seemed to sound not in his mouth but deeper, against the lining of his skull.

He stood still, looking at himself in the mirror, the apparatus hanging from his mouth. It is not too late, he thought, his hand tight on the grips. He looked up, froze. Here was his grandfather at last, startled but attentive, watching him.

Moran's *Mexico*: A Refutation
by C. Stelzmann

Though ostensibly billed as a translation of A. Stelzmann's *Mexico, Kultur- und Wirtschaftkundliches* (Berlin: Otto Quitzow Verlag, 1927), Moran's *Mexico* soon abandons this pretense. Indeed, Moran's English "translation" degenerates from a first-rate travel book into an unnamed narrator's first-person divagations through a countryside possessed of only a marginal similarity to Stelzmann's Mexico. All of Moran's major narrative acts—the unsettling encounter with what the narrator calls the "toothed chamber," the narrator's abandonment of the "unfortunate American," the odd rituals and etiquette practised in the (I believe to be nonexistent) town of Boya—none of these appear in my grandfather's original travelguide. As an individual, my grandfather exhibited no similarity to the wastrel, the gadabout, the indifferent scoundrel proffered as narrator of Moran's so-called translation. Indeed, my grandfather's *Mexico, Kultur- und*

Wirtschaftkundliches eschews the first person pronoun altogether. His travelbook remains consistently third person, objectively rendered. Unlike Moran's, his descriptions of Northern Mexico's culture and people are forever scrupulous, exact.

Moran's text departs from my grandfather's text at the beginning of part ii of the foreword (page 17 of Moran's text, page 16 of the original). Prior to this point the translation, though swollen with minor errors, has conveyed the gist of my grandfather's original. From page 17 onwards, however, translation becomes travesty.

Take, for example, the initial sentence of part ii of the foreword:

> *Das künftige Erfordernis der Weltpolitik ist ein Am-*
> *europa, Ein Amerika-Europa.*

Clear, economical, the statement modestly proffers a defensible position vis-à-vis world politics and the state of the world economy in 1927. Moran translates the sentence as:

> As I was out walking the streets of Laredo, as I was
> out walking Laredo one day, I spied a young Ger-
> man all wrapped in white linen—a linen of Am-
> Euro manufacture, white as Aunt May.

The sentence holds not even the remotest resemblance to my grandfather's original. Only one term, "Am-Euro" is held in common. As for the rest, Moran seems to have forgotten what side of the Mexican-American border a book called *Mexico* should concern—after seventeen pages of introducing Mexico, Moran suddenly offers a sentence which thrusts an unidentified first person narrator, apparently a young German,[1] into a small Texas town. To what end? Who is this young German intended to be? My grandfather, surely, but he is unlike A. Stelzmann in every

---

1. [Translator's Note:] Mr. Stelzmann (the younger) seems to have misunderstood the English original of the sentence, equating the "I" of the passage with the linen-wrapped German encountered. From there, he slides easily into the belief that the young German must represent his grandfather.

particular. What is the significance of his being wrapped in white linen? None of my American encyclopedias or other reference works can proffer an explanation.

Most puzzling of all is the perhaps metaphorical reference to an "Aunt May." My grandfather had strictly Bavarian aunts possessed of strictly Bavarian names (Gretta, for instance, wife of my maternal uncle Klaus Beringer, known for her spaetzle).[2] My research has definitively proven that Moran himself had no Aunt May.[3] The detail seems inserted merely to irritate the reader.

The proliferation of such irritants has caused certain less-than-promising young American jargoneers to wax loquacious over what they call my grandfather's "proto-postmodernism," or his "avant-post-modernism," or even "(pre)(post)modernism." The latter term strikes me as the most apt, but only if the letters "e-r-o-u-s" are inserted between the "t" and the "m." I am proud to say that none of the irritants that compel critics to christen the work postmodern can be blamed upon my grandfather. They are all the work of Moran, inserted into the English revision nearly seventy years after my grandfather first wrote. For this reason they cannot be seen as *proto* anything except the few books written since Moran's *Mexico* was published. Had the so-called scholars bothered to cast even a passing glance at the German original, they would have realized that my grandfather's

---

2. [Translator's Note:] I have inquired of Mr. Stelzmann's cousins, easily accessible through the München telephone guide, who inform me that there is no relative christened Gretta in the family tree. There was a Gretel, wife of Klaus Beringer, but family oral tradition notes her not as an excellent preparer of spaetzle but as an abysmal preparer of all noodle dishes.

When I pointed out to these relatives the disparity between theirs and C. Stelzmann's account, they accused him of having a "vividly revisionary imagination." Indeed, C.'s reputation as a fabulist seemed a source of amusement to them.

3. [Translator's Note:] In fact, Aunt May was the nickname of one of Moran's aunts: Aunt Mabel. The reference to Am-Euro linen, however, is more difficult to sort out, and perhaps is a satirical but obscure jab.

text isn't postmodern *gobblygoo* and *pishradish*.[4] Rather, it is a
genuinely robust travelbook which fits snugly, as all good
travelbooks should, into the confines of its genre. It examines a
particular Central American culture, provides readers with handy
facts and pointers, offers maps to propel tourists from place to
place, and all in all prepares one to pass through an alien culture
unharmed and untouched. The only way one could mistake
Moran's *Mexico* for a translation of my grandfather's book is
through willful ignorance of the original German.

I, on the contrary, unlike the *postmodernescos*, have done
my research. I have returned not only to the original text but to
Moran's copy of my grandfather's *Mexico: Kultur- und
Wirtschaftkundliches*, comparing the twain. This latter I had from
among Moran's very possessions, at great inconvenience and
cost.[5]

---

4. [Translator's Note:] The words *gobblygoo* and *pishradish* are both itali-
cized in C. Stelzmann's original German and may be Stelzmann's attempt to
show himself conversant in authentic American slang. It makes one question Stelzmann's ability with English, makes one wonder if his English is
good enough to properly apprehend the strengths and purpose of Moran's
translation.

5. [Translator's note:] Details of C. Stelzmann's acquisition of said book are
chronicled in a *Stillwater Newspress* article, published January 8 of last year:

Mad German Invades Local Home

Police called to settle what they thought was a
domestic disturbance last night and got more than
they bargained for.

Officer Clive "Jerry" Denkins and Officer Robert
"Jersey" McKay arrived on the scene to discover
the door to the residence ajar, shrieks coming from
inside. They proceeded with caution, with weap-
ons drawn. "We've learned from sad experience,"
said Officer "Jerry" Denkins, "that if you fail to
prepare for the worst in this job, you prepare to
fail."

The kitchen was empty. The bedroom was empty
as well. The officers determined that the shrieking
was coming from what Mr. Moran, the owner of
the home, referred to as "the sunken living room."

The first sixteen pages of Moran's copy of my grandfather's book are meticulously annotated, the margins offering English glosses of German words or phrases. At page sixteen, however, one page before the first eight black and white plates in my grandfather's original, these responsible annotations cease. They are, I regret to say, never to be resumed. Instead, we find Moran writing his own narrative into the margins and directly on the photographs, obscuring the images with his hooked script, as if he is effacing the very world they depict. Which, in effect, he is.

The first eight photographs consist, respectively, of

- a map of Mexico, tracing the path revolutionaries took in 1923 and 1924.
- a map of the world, charting, in one corner, Mexican exports to Europe (imports from Europe to Mexico are not charted).
- an altitudinal map of Mexico, admittedly generalized.
- a map of the highlands of Northern Mexico.

In this sunken living room, a man had been stripped naked. He was gagged, tied to a chair. Another man, in his middle fifties and possessed of an unruly head of hair and a goatee, cavorted around him. He held an open book in his left hand. He slapped the book's pages repeatedly. "He was like some crazed Pentecostal minister," according to "Jersey" McKay. He was screaming in what the two officers at first thought to be gibberish, but which later proved to be the Germanic tongue.

"We thought at first we had walked into some sort of Satanic ritual," suggested Officer "Jersey" McKay.

The assailant, one C. Stelzmann, a German national who had entered the country only a few days before on a tourist visa, is being held for questioning. The owner of the home, Mr. T. Moran, claimed not to know the intruder nor to have any idea of his intentions. Mr. Moran does speak German. He claims the intruder was mad and incoherent, and that he seemed to have mistaken him for someone else.

- a picture of my grandfather's *Tarjeta de identidad* (the 2479th such identity card to be issued if the number stamped into the corner is to be believed). This is my grandfather's only appearance within the text.
- a picture of a *charro*,[6] stray dogs following at his heels as he peers into the window of a train.
- a regional *caudillo* spurring a horse up a steep set of villa steps.
- a cow standing before an old church gate.

The maps and charts and identity card remain unblemished by Moran's pencil, Moran reserving his words to mar the final three photographs, those showing actual scenes from Mexico, though he does blot out the eyes on my grandfather's identity card.

The head of the *charro* is hemmed in by words, his face just preserved through deliberately larger gaps between words. It appears as though he is being smothered by language. Over the train window, slightly larger and in block letters, Moran has written in a speech bubble, "Is this the train to Boya?" The rest of the image—the dogs, the platform, the train—is run over and through by Moran's tiny script, which renders the images just barely discernible. The writing, too, is largely inseparable from the image, sometimes nearly impossible for this reason (and because of the poor handwriting as well) to read.

The picture of the horsed *caudillo* receives similar treatment. Visible, untouched by words, are the pale curve of the horse's neck, the mane above it as well. Barely visible: the seven convex steps of the villa, the balustrade. Threading through the words, an arrow points roughly up the steps. The horse's rider is word-ridden, unblemished only at the elbow, and his face has been

---

6. [Translator's note:] in C. Stelzmann's original the word, in italics, is *churro*, the term for an elongated, sugar-sprinkled Mexican pastry. I have taken the liberty of substituting *charro*, the term he surely meant to use.

drawn over and erased repeatedly until nothing remains except a grayish, dull, ovular absence.

The cow of the final photograph of the series stands dumbly and in profile, head peering back at the camera so that the skin of the neck bunches and folds. The church-gate appears made of stone. It consists of an arch perhaps fifteen feet tall (assuming the cow to be average size), leading, not as one might expect, into a church, but instead into a courtyard of sorts, just a fraction of which is visible. The writing on this page is more controlled, for Moran has chosen to write only on the space within the archway and on the ribs of the cow. Within the arch we find the beginnings of Moran's description of Boya, which appears on page 19 of his "translation":

> The common entrance to Boya is a curious one: one first passes through the court of a partly-walled Church (Roman Catholic, certainly) directly into the plaza. Here one finds a central fountain studded around its basin with a circle of carved stone masks....

And so on. From this description onward, Moran chooses to write exclusively about Boya, his book eschewing Mexico (despite retaining the title *Mexico*) for one town within Mexico. Or, rather, a town claimed to be in Mexico, for Boya makes an appearance on no atlas or map. As far as I have managed to determine, Boya does not exist.

"It is in Boya," Moran has written in minute script on the ribs of the cow, "that you shall meet your wife."

An intriguing presagement. My grandfather did not meet his wife there; he met his wife in Vienna's *Heldenplatz* during a riot of some sort, many years before his voyage to Mexico.[7]

---

7. According to C. Stelzmann's cousins, A. Stelzmann in fact met his wife at a cabaret in Düsseldorf.

Nor for that matter did Moran meet his wife there. His wife, in the few moments I had on the telephone with her before Moran realized to whom she was speaking, confessed to (a) not speaking Spanish, (b) never having gone to Mexico, (c) having been born and raised in Picher, Oklahoma, a small town, so my atlas informs me, in the Northwest corner of the panhandled state[8]: certainly a pleasant midwestern town, white bread and checkered tablecloths, with none of the eccentricities of the imaginary Boya.[9]

Perhaps it is the photogenic cow who will find a wife.[10]

The remainder of Moran's narrative is inscribed upon the pictures and in the margins of Moran's copy of my grandfather's book. Though my grandfather's book totals 293 pages, Moran's *Mexico* amounts to only 122 pages. Apparently Moran hadn't the endurance my grandfather had.

Indeed, the majority of Moran's 122 pages takes place in Boya. After elaborate description of the town and its customs, Moran focuses on three particular locales: the chamber of teeth, the body of a woman, a cave just outside the town.

The chamber of teeth appears on page 27:

---

8. [Translator's note:] C. Stelzmann's original, properly translated, would accuse Oklahoma of being the "panhandling" state, begging perhaps from the other states around it. I have chosen to correct this to both suggest Oklahoma's moniker as "The Panhandle State" and maintain some sense of Stelzmann's odd usage.

9. [Translator's note:] In fact, C. Stelzmann is wrong about Picher; it has at least as many eccentricities as Boya, perhaps more. Picher is a mining town, built up around a series of lead retrieval operations which have left chat piles of chalky, flaky limestone chips throughout the area, some more than 40 feet tall. The mining has left hollow spaces under the town; from time to time the ground will rush out from under a house, the house collapsing, or a child will disappear, sucked under the ground. It is an odd, unearthly town, the landscape grey and moonlike, the population in steady decline.

10. [Translator's note:] C. Stelzmann, who seems to have no knowledge of animal husbandry, does not realize the animal photographed is a cow, a female, and thus not likely to search for a wife.

then Rodriguez put down his glass on the table and
said *Vaminos a la cama de dientes.*

La cama de dientes? I inquired, certain I had
either misheard or misunderstood.

Si, he said, and curling his top and bottom lip
showed me what remained of his own pearly grays.

A few pages later they are walking drunk, the mysterious (and
previously unmentioned) Rodriguez and he, toward the edge of
town. Moran wonders if Rodriguez plans to kill him. Indeed, it
might have been better for everyone involved had Rodriguez
killed Moran;[11] then Moran's *Mexico* would not have come into
existence, and my grandfather's name would have remained
unblemished.

The only reference to a so-called Rodriguez in my
grandfather's original comes underneath a photograph entitled
*Tortilla bereiteren: Tortilla ist der dünne Maisfladen, das Brot
der Bevölkerung*, which shows a young woman grinding corn.
She is perhaps twelve, chubby in the face, her black hair in a
long braid that hangs down one side of her chest. She wears a
spotted blouse and a light-coloured plaid shirt. She is on her
knees on a stone floor, pushing down on a fire-hardened slat
and drawing it over the crushed kernels. Below the picture it
says: *phot. J. Rodriguez, Mexico.* Moran's copy has the name of
the photographer encircled in pencil. Significantly enough, all
that remains unmarred of the girl's picture is her smile, her shining teeth.

Beside the picture, Moran's text continues:

There was at the edge of town, off the road a few
dozen paces, an old and wavering animal track that
was beginning to acquire the characteristics of a

---

11. [Translator's Note:] C. Stelzmann's unstated assumption that the narrator
of the Moran's *Mexico* must be Moran (a revision of the earlier assumption
that the narrator must refer either to his grandfather or to Moran) remains
problematic. There is no convincing textual evidence to suggest that this
must be the case, that the "I" of Moran's *Mexico* is anything but a device.

path. We followed the path through low hills for
perhaps ten minutes, I thinking all the while that
this was mere preparation for my robbery and subsequent murder, yet fascinated and willing to continue nonetheless.

This is resoundingly bad advice for travelers. Moran encour-
ages them to take actions that will cause their throats to be cut.
Suite:

...[T]hen out of the darkness loomed a pale shape,
coming distinct—a house—as we approached.
Rodriguez removed a key from his pocket and
opened the door. Once inside, we fumbled in darkness until he managed to light a candle, a stub of a
thing lying on a table. Holding it carefully to keep
hot tallow from dribbling over his knuckles, he
opened the room's only other door and guided me
into another chamber.

There was something odd about the walls, I
could see from the flickering candle, but it was not
until he thrust the candle near to both the walls
and my face that I saw the wall studded with row
upon row of teeth, some human, most animal. He
took me from wall to wall and, stupefied, I saw
each surface covered with teeth, the room always
at my throat.

The continuation—the coercion of a tooth from Moran himself
for the walls of the room (a lie; when I saw him Moran had all
his teeth)—is of little interest for our purposes.

The woman's house comes next. This story begins in No. 3
pencil beside a drawing entitled *Altmexicanisches Badhaus:
Heizung erfolgt von dem vorgebauten Häusen aus,* which shows
a roundish bathing structure with smoke or steam rising from an
opening in its roof.

Writes Moran, directly on the drawing:

I first made the acquaintance of the woman in the
clapboard house purely by hazard.

—Moran has moved from an image of a bathhouse to an un-
likely clapboard house, either from laziness or from perversity.
He continues—

> I became aware of having lost my pen, a gift from
> Uncle Ferber....

—Moran's genealogy claims no Uncle Ferber, nor does he mention this pen elsewhere in his narrative. My grandfather too had
no such uncle, no such pen—

> ...and wandered back along the path I had taken
> earlier that morning. Keeping my eyes down I man-
> aged to walk right into a woman, both of us tum-
> bling down.

—Too much! We have entered the world of slapstick and unbe-
lievable coincidence, an area already utterly exploited by the
silent cinema. Has the fellow no shame?—

> Soon a friendship was established....

—Note Moran's rapid passage over this event, precisely the useful information one hopes to find explicated in full in a first-rate
travelguide: i.e. how *does* one befriend the natives?—

> ...which led to the shucking of clothing and a most
> unusual incident which I record though I still remain
> a little baffled by what precisely occurred.... [I pass
> over here a long and futile description of the route
> from the fountain of masks to the villa.] At the top of
> the villa steps she began to wax lyrical concerning
> the sexuality of sound, particularly the sound that
> bodies make, the odd ebb and wash that goes on
> beneath flesh. We sat on the steps and she coaxed
> me to lie back until I was flat on the dirt. She placed
> her head against my torso, her ear against my belly,
> and began to describe in telegraphic Spanish what
> she was hearing. After a time she helped me sit again
> and lay back herself, pressing my head to her belly.
> I spoke haltingly of what I heard and she became
> dissatisfied. She asked me to bring my microphone

and a reel-to-reel so as to record the sounds of her
belly and allow her to listen to them herself. When
I indicated that I had no such device, she looked at
me strictly, then left.

I was never to see her again.

What, I ask, does this have to do with Mexico? What possible
connection can be drawn? This is anecdotal information, not useful
to the reader of a travelguide. Indeed, it will give the reader
precisely the wrong idea of what Mexican women are like. Imagine the poor misinformed tourist, bridling his own relatively natural
sexual impulses so as to wander the Sonoran countryside slung
with tape recorder and microphone.

In any case, Moran's story of the woman is patently untrue.
No such woman ever existed, nor is any such woman likely to
exist.[12]

The third incident might be considered unusual were it veri-
fiable. It begins near the end of the book, and seems based
roughly on comments by A. Stelzmann that "there are ample
caves in the hills and mountains of Sonora." Beside this statement, in any case, Moran begins his own incident:

There are ample caves, some of them quite dangerous, as I know from my experiences with the unfortunate American.

---

12. [Translator's note:] C. Stelzmann seems ignorant of the case of Stella
Braun, as mentioned in Merrill-Babb's *Yearbook Annual: 1979*, the supple-
ment to their best-selling *Worldbook Survey*. Miss Braun, it seems, awoke
one morning listening to the beating of blood in her head. Something about
the sound, which she surely had heard many times before without rightly
perceiving it, fascinated her; she found herself with no desire to move. She
was discovered by a neighbor almost twelve days later, in a state of extreme torpor and near death, still intent on listening to her own blood. Only
the white noise of a vacuum cleaner broke the spell. After recovering, Miss
Braun learned to cope with her condition by keeping a radio on and between stations at all times, playing static loudly night and day to silence the
sound of blood.

This "unfortunate American" does not appear either in my grandfather's original nor elsewhere (aside from the cave experience) in Moran's narrative. He is never physically described, never named; little information is offered in connection with him. Critic Simon Bladlock's suggestion[13] that he represents "Arlen Jenkins, an American of middle age" who disappeared in Mexico in early 1927 is not without merit, though Bladlock clearly does not recognize that the incident is not in my grandfather's original text.[14]

> ...We went down the tunnel, the unfortunate American leading the way. We had no torch, though the American did have a gas lighter which he would spin on from time to time so as to gather his bearings. I had a piece of chalk and each time we came to a branching I would mark the wall of the passage we took. Unfortunately, I allowed the American to make the choice each time.

> We came down into a passage that narrowed considerably. I encouraged the American to turn back but he remained convinced that the passage would open up soon. Water was up to our ankles, and we tromped through it, the American now with his lighter on more often than off. We came to a place where the passage angled and narrowed so severely that we had to bend ourselves backward

---

13. [Author's Note:] c.f. Simon Bladlock, "Note: On the 'unfortunate American' in A. Stelzmann's *Mexico*," *Notes and Queries* (Spring 1998): 33-34.

14. [Translator's Note:] According to both the title page of *Notes and Queries* and to Bladlock himself, the title of his paper was "Note: ... Moran's *Mexico*" rather than "Note: ...Stelzmann's *Mexico*." From a letter dated June 1st from Bladlock to the translator:

I have no interest in Stelzmann's text, which I have examined in detail and which, it is clear to me, is no more than an ordinary travel guide. I specifically distinguished between Moran's text and Stelzmann's text in my title and in the text that follows. C. Stelzmann clearly has an agenda: discrediting the Moran text by whatever means possible, including willful distortion of the facts.

and continue by pulling our backs along the rock.
The shirts over our chests were cut by the stone we
scraped past. We could not fully inflate our lungs,
and as we wormed forward we were forced to take
smaller and smaller breaths.

At last, we could move by only bits and starts,
squeezing our way along, pushing our breath completely out and then moving and then drawing
breath back in. The pressure of stone was always
against our backs, our chests. There was the impression of slow suffocation. Then I heard a scraping and the American cried out. Then he flicked on
the lighter and I saw in the wavering light his head
a good foot lower than my own, his legs submerged
to the knees, his chest wedged tightly against the
rock.

"I'm stuck," he said.

"Come back toward me," I said.

"I can't," he said. "My feet aren't touching anything." And then the light flicked off. I reached out
best I could, but could do nothing for him in my
own straited condition.

"Give me the lighter," I finally said.

"Don't leave me," he said, and then, as my hand
tried to take the lighter from his own, "I'll drop it,"
he said. But I already had the lighter in my own
hand and a moment later began to move my way
slowly backward, wriggling my way free. He was
crying out, screaming. Then I was down the other
passages, out in sunlight, back to open air.

I have kept the lighter, a wheel-spun affair, to
this day.

The metaphor is perhaps apt; like the unfortunate American, my
grandfather (admittedly neither unfortunate nor American) has
been left alone in the dark, abandoned by Moran's translation.
We too as readers are left at loose ends, abandoned, benighted
as we try to use Moran's travelguide to navigate the real space of

a real country. We remain wedged in the cave of the text, unable to work our way free and back into living, breathing Mexico.

One might thus aptly conclude this brief study [*Leistungwerk*] with the final image Moran's *Mexico* offers, a photograph tacked on to the end of the narrative, printed on the back cover of the book itself. The photograph is attributed to "Stelz, Mexico," and the caption reads simply "*Das Doppelbild.*" It shows a bare patch of earth, hard and shiny, perhaps a sunlit section of the earthen floor of a house. Across it is spread a shadow. The curve of shoulders and arms, the shape of a torso, the beginnings of a head, are discernible yet distorted, as if the image is either beginning to focus or is coming asunder, moving toward greater collapse. It is for us to determine which it shall be: focus or collapse. Shall we choose the former and allow Moran's *Mexico*, with its constructed narrator, its false town and imagined characters, to stand? Or shall we opt rather to dismember the text so as to see the face behind it, smothered under Moran's words, but still addressing us nonetheless?

The Wavering Knife

I. *Theoria*

Despite the unfortunate and increasingly serious illness of my benefactor, I continued to work without cease or rest to salvage my analysis of the Gengli oeuvre. The image of the wavering knife, which I had for years perceived as the unifier and ultimate hingepiece of Eva Gengli's philosophy, had, under the severe scrutiny made possible by her private papers, collapsed, and I could discover no adequate trope to stand in its stead. Indeed, Eva Gengli's private papers had led me to realize with an alarming degree of clarity that the Gengli philosophy was exceedingly more complex than I had first imagined.

In deference to my benefactor and his declining health, while he was still alive I told him little and in fact nothing of my difficulties. Instead, I continued to serve him as I had before, though hurrying through my assigned tasks so as to spend more time each day with the Gengli papers. Even when I was with my benefactor—undressing him for bed, rubbing his now inadequate legs, reading to him, conversing with him, feeding him, arranging his pillows, undressing him for the night, steadying his walker, propelling him down the hall, preparing his morning meal, reading at him, dressing him for the day, bathing him, preparing his noon meal, ignoring him, preparing his evening meal, straightening the dust ruffle—I was hardly with him at all. Rather, I was with his "lover" (his claim) Eva Gengli's papers, making the most incisive of critical judgements, examining, to give one instance, two versions of Eva Gengli's "Aphorism on Aesthetics," considering which, if either, she meant to be definitive:

> *The ten fingers of the pianist compose the two hands*
> *of the lover.*

or (as marked over in a hand I could not be absolutely certain belonged to Eva Gengli)

> *The ten fingers of the pianist compose the two hands*
> *of the strangler.*

The multiple versions of Eva Gengli's philosophical texts raised difficult questions, made even more difficult by the sense I was gaining that Eva Gengli appeared to regard traditional philosophy as a sort of second-rate game, a game she played well but claimed to have no real stake in. As a result, the philosophical statements she offered were not only variously versioned but were likely to be called into question by what she saw as her more memorable work in film and prose. Nonetheless, I had managed to maintain a firm belief, despite Eva Gengli's own statements, that her philosophical statements were what were genuinely serious.

Admittedly, my task—that of how to salvage and give acclaim to the philosophy while at the same time remaining not unfaithful to Eva Gengli's larger project—had become exceptionally complicated. Since any choice about how to consider an individual philosophical statement first would influence my view of the remainder of the Gengli philosophy and second would demand a continual repositioning in regard to all her work, I was constantly in a state of unease and distress. Worse, rather than establishing a new pattern, each newly considered moment of her philosophy seemed to call into question the hint of pattern I had begun to theorize. Soon I was left only with the trope of the wavering knife and then, as my analysis progressed further, with nothing at all.

I was distracted and despondent for weeks, and grew even more so upon discovering that my benefactor's condition had worsened. The palsification of his body and the dark slur of his speech had grown extreme and could no longer be arrested or corrected by the pharmaceuticals that had lasted us in good stead through the first months of my research. Indeed, my benefactor shook so utterly he could in his worst times no longer raise his hands to his mouth, which meant I had to feed him and even hold his hands and head steady. He could not bear to be left long alone, for alone, he claimed, his condition worsened. He wanted me to stay with him more often, for the severity of the palsy made it difficult and sometimes impossible for him to rest in his bed or in his chair without slipping out, and he would not tolerate the obvious solution of allowing me to strap him in place.

In the seventh month of my analysis, my benefactor's condition had so decayed that he was asking me to drive him again the six hours to his "specialist" (as he referred to his doctor), who, he claimed, would provide the medicines that were sure to make of him "a new man." I was, I must admit, reluctant. It would be a day wasted, I knew, a day that might have in large part been spent in the company of Eva Gengli's papers, trying to unravel from her thought the thread that would allow the unification of her philosophy that I desired. To be away for as long as a day would cause me to lose critical concentration, and to reestablish it again might take weeks. Nor could I envision leaving the Gengli papers unattended, for the house was an old one and could easily be subject to fire and all other manner of calamity, and there were no fire-proof or flood-proof devices that might serve to protect the papers. Worse, the papers could be stolen— for I was far from being the only scholar with an interest in Eva Gengli (though I was the only one to give her philosophy its proper due). There were other scholars who were not as scrupulous as I, who might try to gain access to the papers by dishonest rather than honest means. There were even those who might try to destroy the philosophic papers on the grounds that they obscured the literary work. We could not leave the Gengli papers unattended, I told my benefactor, for to do so would be to shirk all responsibility to philosophy.

At first my benefactor was rather incensed, though gradually he calmed himself enough to set about trying to coerce me to fulfill his will. Immediately seeing through this, I covered my ears and considered the Gengli manuscripts further in my mind, focussing on the tricky problem of "a topography of desire" being substituted for "a trajectory of desire" in the "Flesh" aphorism to describe the intercourse of the mind with the body. The manuscripts made a case for both, my own philosophical bent being better supported if I could discard both statements and think of the mind and body differently. I was thus hoping to discover evidence that the "Flesh" aphorisms had been written at a point of weakness, on a day when Eva Gengli was known to be afflicted or during her rejection of philosophy, when her statements could no longer be trusted. The script in both versions of the aphorism, I recalled, was slightly unstable, and this perhaps could be parlayed into a legitimate, scholarly rejection.

I was well into my mental formulations for dismissal, developing an alternative mind/body formulation, when my benefactor began to jab at me weakly with his cane. Lifting my head, I removed my hands from my ears, showed myself attentive.

"I assume you are ready to listen to reason," he said. He had to say it twice before I was able to draw the meaning out from his slurred and shaking mouth.

"You see the state I am in," he said, his hands bobbing along the coverlet, his head shaking.

I folded my arms across my chest, inclined my head slightly. "It truly injures me to see you this way," I said. This was, in fact, true, though perhaps not in the way he would interpret it.

"I am very ill," he said. "I need my specialist."

I did not disagree with this, though I could not see how his mere *needs* would cause a *duty* to Eva Gengli's philosophy to vanish. Considered objectively, one had a certain obligation (to history, to thought) which demanded sacrifice, which superseded one's immediate pain. Pain must be subsidiary to art, I explained to him, even a function of art itself. Indeed, his "lover" Eva Gengli (if she ever had actually been his lover, which I doubted) had proven this by generating art from pain. Her film sequence "Inscription of the Spastic"—each film one minute long and subtitled after its only subject (e.g. Stephen #5, Helene #12, David P. #19)—had recorded the attempts at movement of forty-two people inflicted with muscular atrophy or spasticity, I reminded him. By recording them, Eva Gengli had transformed pain and dysfunction into something valuable. Privately, I reminded myself that my position was complicated by Eva Gengli's re-editing of the film sequence, her retitling it "Reinscription," and her attempt, by increasing or decreasing the speed of certain moments of the films themselves, to modify each gesture's regularity until it seemed each of the spastic were engaged in a seamless and mysterious dance.

But had not the "Reinscription" been an error in judgement? Was it not better from the philosophical point of view to record pain rather than to regulate it away?

Before I could mount a persuasive mental argument in favor of pain, however, I felt myself prodded again. "If you care to remain in this house," my benefactor said muddily, "you shall obey me."

I quickly stood and passed out of the room. I could hear my benefactor calling behind me, his voice unstable and shaken. I climbed the stairs, went directly to the library. Unlocking the door with the key around my neck, I went in.

With the door shut, I could no longer hear him. The manuscripts were as I had left them, undisturbed. I sat at the table, slid on the cloth gloves, and began to read, following the first text with the index finger of my right hand, the second with the index of my left, my head turning from one text to the other. The first:

> *Aphorism of the Two Enforested Dandies. Nietzsche:*
> *axe. Heidegger: woodpath.*

It was a somewhat odd aphorism which defined a relationship be-
tween two philosophers. "Woodpath" was from Heidegger's work
(*Holzwege*), but I could not remember "axe" having appeared in
Nietzsche's oeuvre and was unsure why it would be paired with
Nietzsche. And why dismiss two radical philosophers as "Dandies"?

Though there was no second version, there did exist a second separate text, a "creative" text. Indeed, the forest scene ex-
cerpted from Eva Gengli's play *The Shadow of a Wing* called the
initial aphorism into question:

> *Ducharme: Nietzsche, he's too busy cutting down*
> *trees to actually pay attention to the forest itself.*
> *Madame Sbro: [clears his [sic] throat]*
> *Ducharme: Yes, it is true. And old Marty Heidegger,*
> *he spends all his time looking for the trees to open*
> *into a clearing so he can spread out his goddamn*
> *picnic.*
> *Madame Sbro: [shaking her [sic] head] And what*
> *about you?*
> *Ducharme: Me? [laughs] I like to spend my after-*
> *noons in the city.*

It is precisely ill-considered passages such as these—passages, I
am convinced, written by Eva Gengli at moments of profound
disturbance late in her life, after a sort of mental decay had begun—which less inventive critics have used to justify a dismissal
of her philosophical statements.

I puzzled over the relation of the two texts for some time in
my head. I considered it in the light of the previous texts I had
encountered, and wrote a summary of the problem on a yellow
legal pad, my seventeenth such pad.

Carefully formulated on paper, the problem began to seem
plain enough, though it was still clear to me, as it had been clear
for some time, that my examination of Eva Gengli's papers was
leading me away from any clean formulation of her philosophy.
This awareness I found to lead to an alternation of despair and
exhilaration. Despair because my analysis was potentially interminable and useless, exhilaration because what I was now doing

was not so much analyzing Eva Gengli's philosophy as entering into it in all its contradiction. I was swallowing the philosophy whole.

After a time, I realized I could hear my benefactor's voice calling me feebly. I opened the door and left the library. Leaning over the banister, I saw my benefactor lying heaped at the bottom of the stairs. I climbed down and picked him up, carried him back to his bedroom. He was trying to speak, but I encouraged him to remain silent until he was lying down and had had a moment to regain his composure. I placed him in his bed, under the blankets and sheets, tightened them around him, safety-pinned them into place to make it difficult for him to shake free again.

"There now," I said. "What would you do without me?"

He coughed, threads of saliva spilling through his lips. His mouth offered something I could not quite understand.

"What?" I asked. "Excuse me?"

"When are you going?" he asked.

"Going?"

"The doctor's."

"I am just leaving," I said. I kissed him on the forehead, then returned directly to the library, resuming my analysis where I had left off.

By the time I had reached the point where I could conveniently arrest my research, it was well past midnight. I arranged the books, secured the door to the library. I went downstairs, turning off the lights on my way.

Passing my benefactor's door, I heard him groan. I went inside. He was out of his bed again and crumpled in the corner, shaking violently. He had overturned the telephone table and had a puffy gash across his forehead, the skin all around it dull and abnormally raised. The telephone receiver was in his hand, the black cord entangled all around his forehead in a sort of dark nimbus, the base wedged somehow underneath his legs.

I carefully disentangled him and carried him back to his bed.

"The medicine?" he asked.

I ignored him, set about arranging his bed.

"You have it?" he asked.

"What you need is a good long sleep," I said.

I left him and went into the bathroom. Removing a bottle of sleeping pills, I shook a half-dozen into my hand. Filling an empty medicine bottle with tapwater, I returned to my benefactor's room.

"Take these," I said. "They will make you feel better."

"I don't want to fall asleep," he claimed.

"It's time to sleep," I said. I showed him the clock on the bureau. "You see?" I said. "This is for your own good."

In the end I had to force his jaws open and push the pills down his throat one by one, as one is sometimes forced to do with cats. He choked a little, but in the end swallowed everything.

"What did you do to the telephone?" he asked.

"The telephone?" I picked up the receiver, listened to the absence of any dial tone. "I know nothing about it," I claimed.

He looked blearily up at me.

"What are you planning to do with me?" he asked.

"Nothing," I said. I smiled to reassure him. "I am here only to serve."

II. *Zwischen*

Somewhere in the space between my analysis of the 128th aphorism (variously titled the "Aphorism on Adultery" and "Aphorism on Adulthood") and my return to Eva Gengli's only extended philosophical text, *A Blotter of Wings*, my benefactor's condition worsened considerably. He lost the ability to move of his own accord and will, individual portions of his body and speech having altogether fled his frame. His eyes, when I opened them with my fingers, stumbled about the sockets. He was having difficulty breathing and the shuddering of his body was so severe it seemed as if he would shake the flesh off his bones.

It was difficult to conduct a proper philosophical investigation under such circumstances, and had I not been intent on beginning an analysis of *A Blotter of Wings* I would have temporarily set all philosophy aside. Yet I had been struggling to gain an approach to *A Blotter of Wings* for months. At one time I had thought to have found, in the trope of the wavering knife, the proper and perhaps only unified approach to the book, the device that would lay bare certain fundamental consistencies of Eva Gengli's thought and make it manageable. But as I looked closer, I realized that Eva Gengli could not be reduced to fundamental structures or strictures, that her philosophy simply refused to conform to "thought" as I understood the term. Perhaps, I thought, the wavering knife could be coupled with another trope, or perhaps with a series of tropes—the rapid beating of insect wings, for instance (c.f. 34), or the overlayering and interlarding of faces suggested on page 21, or even the strange notion of the soul as container for the body, as existing not embedded in the flesh, but as a membrane between flesh and the world (83-97). Perhaps, I tried to believe, by beginning with Eva Gengli's abandonment of interiority ("the mind," she claimed, "is merely an image among others, a moment of vision"), one might be able to impose a structure that would at least allow the analysis to be written. Though I suspected in advance this would fail, I attempted it anyway. I wrote through the night and well into the day with an increasing sense of hopelessness, a hopelessness that eventually grew strong enough to cause me to tear to shreds the sheets I had written and sit for a further seven or eight hours staring at a blank piece of paper.

I might have sat in the same position for another seven or eight hours except that I began to grow hungry and, growing hungry, realized that I had not fed my benefactor for several days. Going downstairs, I found him with his legs still on the bed and entangled in the blanket, his body hanging out, his head and face pushed against the floor. I lifted him up, found his pulse torpid, his skin cold to the touch. I shook him a little, spoke to him even, but he would not move.

I straightened him on the bed. Going upstairs to the library, I surveyed the careful piles and stacks of Eva Gengli's papers. I was, I considered, now that my benefactor was apparently incapacitated beyond the ability to make decisions, the sole caretaker of all that remained of Eva Gengli. Carefully, I gathered her papers back into the boxes they had been kept in before I had volunteered my service to my benefactor. I piled the boxes at the bottom of the stairs, then loaded them one by one into my benefactor's automobile, always holding my eyes both to the boxes in the automobile and to the boxes still piled just inside the door. I could of course not observe both at once, but looked rapidly from one to another, switching my gaze with such speed that it was as if I were observing both at once. The boxes filled the trunk and all but the front seat of the "mini-sedan" (as the manufacturers shamelessly had chosen to name the vehicle), except that when I tried to close the trunk it would not close, so two boxes did have to go in the front seat as well. *A mini-sedan!* I thought. *How could the incomparable Eva Gengli ever have been involved with someone who owned a mini-sedan?* It was a disservice to her memory to put her papers into such a car, but unfortunately I had no choice.

My benefactor, I further considered, was a small, slight, rat-like person—not at all the sort I would imagine Eva Gengli to involve herself with, though exactly the sort of person who would choose to drive a mini-sedan. But here, now, in the box-cramped car, perhaps I could use my benefactor's slightness to my advantage. In his present condition, perhaps I could wedge him between a box and the door to steady him and keep him aright, and use the other box to rest his feet upon. In his present condition, he was in no condition to object. I would make him fit.

After locking all the automobile doors, then checking again to assure myself they were locked, I went back into the house. My benefactor was on the bed where I had left him, still unconscious, his body slightly tremulous. I gathered him up in my arms and carried him out. Unlocking and opening the automobile door, I forced him inside, pushing his knees up near his chest and working him sideways until he was in. He fit nicely as long as I kept his knees folded up and against his chest. Getting into the automobile, I worked the key.

Though the automobile had not been driven in months it started cleanly, which I saw as a blessing from the Gengli muse, as it were, a ratification of my impulses. Pulling from the drive, I moved down the road, away from town.

A mile from the highway, I pulled the automobile onto a farm route and passed out through fields already thick with grain, past farmhouses, satellite dishes, hulks of ruined automobiles. The road curved and splayed and turned into gravel, and we passed underneath the highway, passed a ruined and gutted and defaced building, a shattered circle of concrete around it, moving deeper into the country. The road turned dirt, becoming rutted and hard. I was forced to shift the gear downward which, because of the boxes, was no easy task.

Near a cornfield, I eased the mini-sedan to the edge of the track and switched it off. My benefactor, I saw, was no longer shaking or moving at all. His tongue was pushing slightly from between his lips. I reached across the seat, forced his knees further apart. I pressed my fingers into his neck. Along the web of my thumb, I could still feel something of a pulse to him. When I separated his eyelids, the eye remain dilated, settling slowly lower in the socket as I shook him.

Putting my hands more firmly around the neck, I squeezed. His neck and shoulder crumpled into the seat, his chin pressing hard against my wrist. He hardly moved, only fluttering his hand a little, and when he was perhaps already dead his eyes opened and clouded slowly, the pupil fading dull. I shook my hands loose, smelled them. They did not smell like anything. I climbed out of the automobile and got him out too, dragging him out into the weeds. Locking the doors, keeping always one eye on the mini-sedan containing the boxes of Eva Gengli's private papers, I dragged the body out into the cornfield, smoothed the arms down along the sides as my impulses directed me to do. I examined my handiwork.

It was utterly clear to me now that Eva Gengli had meant in her "Aphorism on Aesthetics" the two hands of the strangler, not the two hands of a lover. That had been correct.

I had made a mistake in trying to limit my analysis to the

page, I thought. Theory can only take one so far. Praxis is everything. One understands nothing until one begins to act.

III. *Praxis*

When I entered again, the house itself was mostly dark and quiet, the air still but for the dust and hair aswirl near where I had dropped the boxes, dust rising from my footsteps as well. I climbed the stairs and switched on the library lights, found everything as undisturbed as I had left it. I moved through the house, switching on lights, looking into each room to assure myself that I was in fact alone with Eva Gengli.

In my benefactor's room I smoothed the sheets, fluffed the pillow to remove from it the crease of his head. I stood back to admire my handiwork but, seeing the crease still to remain somewhat, I stripped the bed of sheets, balling them up and hiding them in the kitchen, under the sink. I considered the sink for some time, then took the sheets and hid them inside the refrigerator. I looked at the refrigerator a while, then took the sheets out and pushed them out the kitchen window.

There was still the smell of my benefactor in the room and through the entire house. I could not stop myself from fitting rubber gloves over my hands and walking about the house spraying disinfectant/deodorant aerosol before me, feeling it settle tingling on my arms. In a little while I could hardly breathe, so stripped off the gloves and abandoned both them and the disinfectant/deodorant, pushing them out the kitchen window.

I carried my lover's boxes upstairs to the library, one after the other. I was prepared to unpack them, but my forearms, I found, were sticky with disinfectant/deodorant, and the rubber gloves had made my hands watery. It would be an error, I thought, as well as a show of disrespect, to touch Eva's private papers in such a condition.

Going downstairs, I began to lather my hands in the bathroom basin. The lip of the sink and the floor below, I observed as I scrubbed, were clottered over by dark strands of my benefactor's hair. I rinsed and dried my hands, then swept the hair over the edge with my forefinger, gathering it in my other palm, then got on my knees and plucked it up strand by strand until the bathroom was mainly bald and hairless. I chartered the remainder of the house on my knees, the crease of my palm tight with hair, looking for further remnant of my benefactor. There was hair, I saw, everywhere, and dust too, and perhaps in the dust flakes of skin, and perhaps, I could not help but think, the dust was entirely made of flakes of skin. But the difficulty was in sifting and sorting, in separating the skin of my benefactor from what might still remain of Eva Gengli's "uncannily soft skin" (my benefactor's claim, though I doubt he would have ever touched it). Looking at the hair in my hand I noticed among it one or two strands of lighter hair, perhaps blond, perhaps white—perhaps her very hair, though she had died years before. I unthreaded these hairs, slipped them inside my shirt. The remainder, the dark strands, I took to the window and abandoned to the outside.

There was a scent still but no longer so strong. If I concentrated I could ignore it entirely. Indeed, there was little enough of my benefactor left and what was left was spread thin enough that I could feel through it and alongside it, in the stillness, something else entirely. What remained no longer was my benefactor refusing death but the force of a stronger mind, of my lover Eva Gengli gathering her breath just for me.

I moved quickly up the stairs to the library. Throwing the lids off the boxes, I arranged Eva's manuscripts in a circle all around me. Taking the pen, I poised it over a blank page. I waited for her to speak.

She, Eva Gengli, I began, *fighting a too uncanny sense of the presence of her own body, turned for a brief moment to philosophy for solace. In the short form, the aphorism in particular, she found a means of moving from a palpable space to a uniquely regenerative cerebral space. She, however—wrongly this critic believes—always dismissed her philosophical musings in general and her aphorisms in particular, claiming that they were useful as a means of "drawing breath" so as to return to her "only important work, the novels and films" (her words). The philosophy, she claimed in her famous but perhaps unfortunate letter to A. Kline, was "a temporary relief from the body," a sort of "necessary and necessarily ephemeral affair," afterwards allowing her to return more strongly to "the dark or bright bond between writing and flesh."*

Despite the strength of the aphorisms, I wrote, *it is Gengli's single extended treatise, with its exploration of pain and its critique of all dichotomy, that marks her as among the greatest philosophers of her generation. In this treatise,* A Blotter of Wings, *Eva Gengli postulates through the unifying image of the wavering knife (the knife wavering so rapidly as to resemble a beating pair of insect wings) that—*

My inspiration had suddenly fled altogether.

I put my pen down and went downstairs to see if the door was locked. It was locked. There was a smell to the house still, I now noticed. I went into the kitchen to gather the gloves and disinfectant/deodorant, but the space they normally occupied was empty. I opened the kitchen cupboards, closed them again. I opened the stove, pushed my head in, withdrew it.

Upstairs again, I read over what I had written. I had fallen back on the wavering knife despite knowing from my protracted analysis of Eva Gengli's work that the trope would not hold. Insisting upon it as a unifier, I told myself, would lead to a tremendously faulty reading of the Gengli philosophical oeuvre. And there was nothing of Eva Gengli in my writing either, I now realized. My style was turgid, nothing like the flowing and lucid prose of my lover, the careful repetitions ringing like dark chimes, words spilling slick as blood off the tongue. With every word I was writing about Eva Gengli, I realized, I was in fact betraying her. This might have been acceptable were I in fact betraying part of her, the "creative" part, to forward the philosophy, but only a dozen sentences in it was already clear to me that I was betraying all portions of her, and her mind and body too.

I tore the page up and carried it downstairs, dumped the scraps out the kitchen window. Taking a new, unblemished page, I sat down, attempted to begin again.

She, Eva Gengli, I wrote, *overwhelmed by her own touch, turned her gaze rational for an instant and rendered her hand philosophical. It was during this transition, between her novel* A Tergo *and her play* The Shadow of a Wing, *that Eva Gengli did her finest and—*

That was not it, not it at all. Although my benefactor had mostly fled the house, all his possessions were still present. They were pushing against the walls, limiting the air of the house, stifling and strangling what still remained of the woman he claimed had been his lover (Eva Gengli: impossible!).

I went through the shelves of the library, sorting out all those books which Eva Gengli had not signed inside the front cover. I carried each armload of books downstairs and dumped it out the kitchen window, the books cascading off the back porch and onto the lawn. There were, I saw on my tenth trip, neighbors and others of the curious beginning to gather, all of whom I ignored.

When the library had been cleansed sufficiently of all non-Gengli-related texts, I went back in and sat in it again. I closed my eyes, listened. Though it would be untrue to say I felt the presence of my lover Eva Gengli as clearly as I had when I was first compelled to begin, I did not feel my benefactor at all anymore, until I sensed him seeping under the library door from the other parts of his house where his possessions were still abundant.

I took off my shirt and tried to cram the crack under the door shut with it, but it was not long enough so I had to remove my pants as well. When I was done, I stared at the stuffed crack for about an hour, sniffing at it, then tried to write. Nothing at all was coming. My lover had abandoned me.

Pushing the clothing aside and opening the door, I went downstairs. The air outside the library was fetid, marauded through with smells that worked against the purpose of true scholarship. I went around the house, throwing open windows until halfway around, seeing the neighbors crouched about outside, observing me, I realized that perhaps what was outside the house was worse than what was in. At least with the windows closed nothing new could enter. I went about the house closing the windows again, thinking that what I needed now was a system or method to keep at bay all that was undesirable, and to clean the air for thought.

The technique I first employed was incendiary. I went from room to room striking matches, the sweet burn of sulfur ridding the air at least for a moment of the smells of my benefactor's dying (now dead) body, a rat-like body which I was certain Eva could never have touched. Yet matches were not sufficient; all his things were still in the house. As soon as a match was damped out, the things themselves tried to fill the room again before good air could rush in and fill the gap. I was moving about the house striking matches as quickly as I could and dropping them and letting them burn themselves out, but nothing permanent was happening except for the floorboards smouldering in some parts, so that I had to stamp the sparks out with my bare feet until the soles of my feet were slicked dark and burnt a little.

I figured there had to be a better way. I could hardly write my analysis while running about striking matches. So instead of the matches I began to move things out again, starting first with things in plain sight that my benefactor had valued, such as the half-meter cactus, the bronzed shoe, the handsewn tablecloth, the Senegalese mask. I moved them into the kitchen and threw them out the kitchen window. What would not fit out, I broke up until it would fit and then threw out. Once I had finished with the incidentals, I began to try to move the furniture out. Only I could not, with the tools available to me, think of a way to break things like the couch and bed into small enough pieces, so left them jumbled in the kitchen while I ruminated over their possible means of expulsion and went in search of easier prey.

I had begun to dispose of the clothing from my benefactor's closet when, in the back of it, wrapped in brown paper, I discovered a dress. It was black mostly, with a nearly hidden abstract patterning similar to a dress Eva had worn on the back cover of her *Lead Glass Iris*.

Confronted by my lover's dress, I suddenly was conscious again of my own nakedness. I began to put on one of my benefactor's suits, but before it was all the way on I could feel that it would not sit easily on my skin. I removed it and tried another, then another, until the whole of the room was scattered with his clothing and the only thing untried still was the dress.

I shook it out, slipped it over my head. It was tight but would fit mostly if I did not button it and did not move my arms too far. It felt good on me, the fabric smooth, of an odd, subtle weave. I could not stop running my hands over it.

I looked at myself in the mirror. I was so lovely I could hardly recognize myself. I looked in the drawers for something to put my face back on, but there was nothing. I was so lovely I could hardly bear to look at myself, and I could not stop my hands caressing or my mouth from speaking her name.

I could feel her all around me like a sheen over the surface of my body, and she having taken charge of me as well. I could see her gathering in my reflection. The whole world was turning and me along with it, and I was falling backwards and onto the floor, so taken with everything I could not move except in response to her missing touch, all language and analysis having fled me, my dress coming off, my lover's body touching all parts of my body until my body too was wavering and coming asunder and my soul dissolved and expelled to bubble along the surface of my skin and away, until nothing was left of myself nor my body, nothing left of anything at all.

Calling the Hour

I.

One hand full, the other hand empty, both hands gone full as he grasped the back of his shirt, stripped it fluidly off over his head, the shirt dropping and the same hand hovering at her own chest, parting the buttons of her shirt, then tugging the shirt back and down by the collar until it hung just above her elbows like a wrap now, shoulders bare. He let the collar go and one hand fell empty again and moved to draw her in, she too startled to resist the half-nude embrace: the warm dry feel of chest against shoulder, arms wrapped about her, empty hand flat and spread flat across her back, full hand all knuckled up around the gun and granching against her side. She still could not move at the cessation of the embrace, might never have moved had it not been for him now tugging her before the mirror, his arm around her shoulders, drawing her in and tight until they both stood configured in the silvered glass from shoulders up, shoulder to shoulder, both seemingly bare, her neck blotching now, his arm drifting over now to drape fingers over her ear. And then his gunless hand pulling their heads together, pressing ear to ear as she watched still in the mirror, his other hand now rising to lift the gun to his own temple, aiming through his head at her own. She observed the flattened image steady the pistol, press it hard against the free side of his skull, cock, fire.

II.

Face no more than a dark blur at first and then still a blur but clearer. The other man behind her, holding her head at the temples and forcing it forward, demanding she regard what he claimed to be her reflection. There, in the bright pocked metal: the shaved temple, the dark blister of blood where a fragment of bullet had passed through his head and touched hers. *Perhaps any number of heads*, she thought—*hardly my head,* she thought, as the other man spoke urgently and psychiatrically at her, at the odd, blurred visage in the metal tabletop which she could not accept as her own. It was his visage she was looking at, she realized of a sudden, his preserved head: she knew the other side of the head where the bullet had burst forth was a ruin, would be a ruin still, but she did not dare turn her head to see. If she does not turn her head she can still consider herself to be herself head to tail even if her head is his head, even if she does not know the whereabouts of his bony body, wandering and armatured with her own head.

III.

He now roamed woman-faced, now exulant and incognito while she has ended up male-visaged and always in danger of collapse, always just seconds before the sound of the gun as it goes off, the burn of powder and the pain in the head as she falls, her doubled image gone bloody and slipping from the mirror. They are calling the hour now, the other man long gone from behind her, the nightwatchmen coaxing her up from the table and down the shadowed hall, a final vision pursuing her now and catching at her heels, ephemerated movements and discerpted forms spinning along fresh-polished floors. She knows it is the cast of her own legs and feet she is seeing, the feet of the nightwatchmen as well, perhaps here and there glimpses of her head and other parts. But there seems more than that, a supplemental furzing of shadow and color which she knows as the coming into being of his peculiar vision: soon in the shadows of her room, the locked door, the steps of nightwatchmen crossing up and down halls, the vision will nearly claim discrete shape. His form a dim phantasm intorting in the shadows of the room, congealing and fading over the night's course. She shall rise from the bed to try to capture him in her blanket, try to retrieve her head, but each time she believes to have him he will reveal himself just over her shoulder, laughing with her voice, her lips, as she herself knits his furrowed brow and tries again. Then, later, morning, the blanket empty, the door snapping open and she will be drawn back down the corridor again into the same day she has just left, knowing at both ends of the corridor he shall await her, full- and empty-handed, and no place for her to turn but toward him.

Virtual

I.

Well after the death of his child, abandoned by his wife and sunk into a despair lasting the better part of a year, Rudy discovered the album. His wife had hidden it on the third shelf of the linen closet, under a pile of sheets. A note tucked inside the front cover wished him a *good life, just to remind you by God here is all you've lost.*

The note he left shelved, between sheets. The album he made the mistake of taking out, carrying to the table, opening.

Inside, a series of photographs: himself, his wife. There were baby clothes too in many of the pictures, spread over his arm or smoothed across his wife's shoulder. In one picture, his wife held a tightly rolled blanket. Beside it, a picture of himself holding the same blanket and peering down the end of it, smiling. There he was, sitting at a picnic table, arms around empty air, and there again, crowded into the right half of the photograph, squatting, arm propped out, hand kneading empty air.

This is the version he initially told himself, the version he grew comfortable with but also the version which, as he told it over, he began increasingly to doubt:

One October, the child was stillborn, five months early, less a birth than a spontaneous expulsion of blood. By December, his wife was imagining life back into the child. She began patting her stomach, waddling about as if her belly were still distended.

Rudy didn't know what to say. He understood that there was something seriously amiss, the world had slipped out of joint. Yet there was a glow to his wife again, her skin, her eyes. Watching her, despite himself, Rudy was tempted to join in.

In January, she asked him to speak to the baby, to rest his throat against her belly and talk to the fetus. *Absolutely not*, he said.

She wept for what struck him as an interminable length of time. He didn't love her, she informed him, let alone the baby. This apparently rendered him heartless. When he declared there was no baby, she grew hysterical. She broke plates as long as there were plates to be broken, then stopped cold.

When he asked her if she was all right, *Why shouldn't I be?* she claimed. *Where did this come from?* she asked, staring at the shards scattering the kitchen floor.

When, a day later, she asked him to address her belly, Rudy suggested she seek counseling. She accused him of not loving the baby. When he said there was no baby to love, she had a go at clawing off his face. He dragged her out to the car by the hair, forcing her down onto the floorboards and pushing down hard on the back of her neck with his hand. He drove bent over, just able to see over the dashboard. By the time he reached the hospital, she was calm. He hauled her out, an old lollipop and fluffs of lint in her hair. He took her through the doors and checked her in, sat with her in the waiting room until they finally dredged up an intern to speak with her.

The intern palpated her stomach. "Why do you think you're having a baby?" he asked.

Rudy's wife looked at the man carefully and seriously. "But I think nothing of the sort."

"Your husband suggested—"

"We had a misunderstanding," she said. "My husband brought me here over a misunderstanding."

Rudy could not keep from breaking in, trying to explain the situation, how she was. He had no intention of committing anyone, he said, he just wanted advice. The intern regarded him fiercely, then turned to Rudy's wife.

"Do you need shelter?" he asked her.

Rudy shut up. He was glad when she said no, that he was not abusive, that it was just a misunderstanding. He remained silent, listened to her as she answered the intern's questions impeccably, as if she were actually sane. Eventually, the intern asked him to wait in the hall. When she came out her eyes were red. There was nothing to do but put her back in the car. She spoke about the baby all the way home, rubbing her belly.

After the third trip to the emergency room, Rudy stopped taking her. There was still a glow to her, he conceded, exhausted, almost as if she actually were having a child. She had tremendous energy. She painted the spare bedroom sky-blue, applying puffs of cloud to the walls with a sponge. She came home with brightly colored and simple toys, a mobile, a secondhand crib, small pastel outfits, a changing table, two sheafs of disposable diapers. She spoke constantly about the baby, speculating about which one of them it would resemble. *Names:* she said, *I prefer Corey myself, but what will they call him when he's grown up? Corey's hardly a name a man can bear all his life.*

He let her speak. There was little he could do, at least that he was willing to do, to stop her. She expected no response even when she framed a question to him. The only moments he still had difficulty were when she asked him to speak to the baby, to place his throat against her belly so as to let the baby feel the vibration of his voice. That, she did expect of him. *If you don't speak to him, how will he know you when he's born?* she asked. She kept asking, begging him to speak to the baby, until finally he was obliged to say something. *It won't be born*, he would say, or *There is no baby*. Then came a fit, until at last he shut himself into the bathroom with a book, turned on the fan, tried to read while she banged and frothed outside the door.

They were having trouble, she said to him the last time he came out of the bathroom. She needed to talk frankly for once. Their marriage was collapsing. Didn't he want this baby? It happened to a lot of couples, she confided, she had read about it. A baby changed everything; it took some getting used to. The one thing he couldn't do, though, was stay in denial. If he couldn't face up to the fact of the baby now, before the birth, how would he face the actual baby?

I am living with a crazy person, he had thought. But later, after she was gone, flipping through the album, he wasn't certain about this either.

She understood it was difficult, she said. She wasn't the perfect spouse. She had her own set of problems, true, but she'd been good to him, no? *A marriage was something that involved two people*—probably something she'd heard on TV earlier that week—*and both people had to give a little if the marriage was to succeed*. That was particularly true now, she said, in a time fraught with the changes due to the baby's imminent arrival. She lifted her shirt, thrust her flat belly at him. *If you won't for Baby*, she said, *do for me*.

Despite himself, he did.

The birth occurred while Rudy was at work. He came in to find his wife smiling. When he pulled up her shirt to speak to her belly, she tugged the shirt back down again.

"Don't be silly," she laughed.

He was glad for the respite, thought for a bare moment that she had swung back to her senses. He poured himself vodka and tonic, sat down. She returned to stirring a pot on the stove, steam rising from it.

"What's for dinner?" he asked.

"Nothing much," she said.

He rose and went to her, pressed his chest against her back. Over her shoulder he could see a pot full of roiling bottle nipples.

"What are those?"

"What, these?"

"In the pot," he said.

She giggled. "Don't be silly," she said. "You know what those are. They're for the baby."

"The baby?"

She walked into the spare bedroom, returned with a swaddled blanket carefully tucked into the crook of her arm.

His first thought was that she had stolen a baby. He held still so as not to startle her. He let her come close, watched her hold the swaddled form out.

"See?" she said. "Spitting image of his father."

He poked the blanket. His finger met no resistance. There was nothing there—a fold of blanket, a crease where a baby's face might ride athwart the blankets, nothing else.

"Careful," she said. "There, now you've made him cry."

But he could hear only his wife's crying, her solitary sound. She walked about the room, shaking the pile of blankets softly, cooing at it. "We'll be up all night now," she said, voice tight, brisk. "Fix up a bottle."

"Darling," he said. "Listen. There isn't any baby."

"We'll name him after you," she said, quickly. She was holding the blanket oddly cradled, as if it were bigger than it was. "Rudy Junior," she said.

He turned about in a circle away from her and toward her and away from her again. "Stop," he said. "For God's sake, stop."

"Stop what?"

He took hold of the blanket. He began to tug at it softly. She began to keen, low at first and then high and desperate as the fabric slipped bit by bit from her hands. Then the blanket rested in his hands alone and her hands cupped air, her breath coming and going in gasps.

"He nearly fell," she said.

"There's nothing there," he said. He shook out the blanket, dropped it to the floor.

She was still making a cradle of her arms. He stepped toward her and she turned cringing from him, hiding the absence behind her body. "Come any closer, I call the police," she said. "You're crazy," she said.

"But," he said, "there's nothing there."

"I want a divorce," she said, tugging at her dress with her free hand.

He stared at her, moving his jaws slightly. "You what?"

"You heard me," she said. "You heard."

"No," he said. "Not, I don't, but—"

"You heard," she said. "Leave."

Looking back, Rudy felt that that was the decisive moment in the relationship. *Leave,* she had said, and he had left the house. He walked the neighborhood, slowly and methodically examining cedar and picket and chain-link fences. Several houses down, a retarded girl sat on her parents' porch, wearing a Walkman, pretending to listen to a cordless phone through the Walkman's headphones. He looked at the facades of houses. He walked up to the next corner and stayed watching the cars pass, the motel's sign flickering a half mile distant. Then, having nowhere to go, he turned around, returned home.

His wife stood at the stove, stirring a pot, steam rising from it. Holding the door open, he regarded her back.

She took the spoon from the pot, knocking it twice against the pot's lip, then set it beside the burner. She turned her cheek toward him for a kiss. Her face was untroubled as glass.

"How was work?" she asked.

He nodded slightly, regarding the spoon. He put his arms against her.

"It's nice to see you," she said.

He cleared his throat. He patted her on the back. Then she was out of his arms, head cocked to one side.

"Did you hear something?" she asked.

"No," he said.

"I'm sure I did," she said. "Put together a bottle for him, will you darling?"

He opened his mouth, but did not speak. He watched her go through the door, into the room with sky-blue walls. He stood

awkwardly, then slowly made his way to the stove, fished a
bottle nipple out of the pot with the spoon. Holding it balanced
on the spoon's curve, he awaited her return.

II.

And then in the album came a different period. In those
photos, he could see the child. There, a photo of Rudy sur-
rounded by gifts, the child in his arms. He could actually see the
child in that photo and the photos that followed, just a baby at
first, perhaps three months old, then a toddler, then older still. It
was this that made the version he first told himself seem false.
Perhaps whatever had been wrong with him was wrong with
him still. If the baby was in these photographs, he told himself, it
must be in the earlier pictures as well. Yet when he turned back
the stiff cardboard pages to the earlier photographs, he saw no
child.

By his own birthday, he had begun to see the baby. He was
sick, he felt, something gone amiss with him. He didn't care. At
first it was intermittent. He would see the baby only in the presence of his wife, only when the two of them were alone. The
child was transparent, hallucinatory, the image fading and rising.
He could never fully gather its face, though his wife claimed it
resembled him. Taking the baby in his arms, he could see it but
not feel it. He watched it float against his chest, legs kicking
slightly, then silently handed it back.

Seeing the baby marked the beginning of a period where he
seemed to live two lives at once, one compressed and rapid, the
other slowed, stretched. In the first were his wife and child, the
baby growing at what seemed a remarkable rate. The growth was
always announced by his wife and not seen by him at first, but
then quickly there. The baby crawled today, she would say, and
then he would see it, the baby no longer lying on its back with its
legs quickening the air, but scooting madly all about the house.

The baby seemed to grow faster than he expected, crawling in what seemed to him little more than a few weeks. This, his wife assured him, was *the normal time*, perhaps even a little slow. He watched her face as she said it, but learned nothing.

Indeed, it struck him that he and the baby were growing at different rates, on two separate tracks of time. Or, rather, he stepped back and forth between the track of time found only within the house and the track outside, constantly speeding and slowing, perpetually off balance.

In the second life, the slower track, was the rest of his life, all that he did not touch. His work, time spent with colleagues, seemed interminable. His sleep, too, was on the slow track, and often he awoke with the impression that his wife and child had slept four or five nights for every night of his. Colleagues and coworkers noticed a change in him, accused him of looking beleaguered. He was distracted at work, mistrusted his experience outside the house. His supervisor called him in, called attention to his numbers. He had done Rudy the kindness of displaying his numbers on a tri-color graph. On the top was written "Roy's Numbers." Rudy had to admit they were appalling. He wracked his brain, trying to determine if there was a person employed by the company named Roy. The supervisor gave him a copy of the graph to keep, along with a tri-color "goal graph," then asked,

"How are things at home, Roy?"

"Rudy," said Rudy.

"Ruddy, you mean?" said the supervisor. "In what sense are things at home ruddy? Frankly, you're not using the word in a way I understand, Roy."

Had he become Roy in this life? He wanted to get out his wallet, look at his driver's license, assure himself of his name.

"It's the baby," said Rudy.

"Ah," said the supervisor. "I hadn't even realized your wife was expecting."

Rudy nodded. "It's more work than I realized."

He was given an informal reprimand. *I'm not even going to write you up, Roy.* He felt guilty about having used the baby as an excuse, but when he went home he found the baby *ruddy*, color to it, body, more substantial than before. For the first time, muffled, as if from a distance, he heard its voice.

For the next few weeks, his coworkers congratulated him on the happy arrival—they were surprised, they said, to know he had a baby: why had he said nothing? There were handshakes, small inconsequential gifts, several candied and one actual cigar.

"So, when are we going to see the bundle of joy?" one of them wanted to know, a short dumpy woman from accounting.

Rudy looked around at the things on his desk. He couldn't come up with anything to say.

"You'll bring him in?"

"Sure," said Rudy. "Sometime."

"How about later in the week?"

"Sure," he said.

But how could he join two tracks of time? Was it even possible?

That evening, in darkness, he told his wife that people wanted to see the baby.

"No," she said. "I don't think so. The workplace place is a haven for germs."

He nodded slightly. He got up from bed, went to the sky-blue room, looked into the crib. The child was there, lying in the crib, unmoving, eyes wide open. It did not blink. He picked it up and immediately it began to blink and stretch, mumbling softly. It seemed to be looking at his face. He put the child back down. Instantly it was static again.

"How's the baby?" he heard his wife say behind him. "Everything all right?"

"I don't know," he said, somewhat puzzled.

She leaned against the crib rail, one breast pressing flat. "Look," she said, "he's sleeping." When he looked again there was the baby, eyes wandering slightly beneath the lids, chest falling up and down, the most natural thing in the world.

He put them off at the office for well over a year, until they began to question whether he really had a baby at all. *At least bring pictures,* the girl from accounting insisted, but his wife would not allow even this, though she would not say why. He found he had some anxiety about the pictures as well, but could not make sense of it until later, well after his wife had left him, when he spent several days without eating or sleeping, on the couch, staring at the album.

It had been almost a year and a half since the birth. The baby was growing, bigger and more coordinated than he thought a baby should be at that age. Indeed, he remembered having held three birthdays for the child. It was something he couldn't sort out, life somehow moving at a different pace inside his house. He knew it would not be wise to inquire into it too closely. He went to work, operating in a sort of daze, keeping the accuracy of his numbers just above the minimum the supervisor demanded. Then he would go home, listen to his wife speak about what the baby had done, the child changing shape and size and coloration before his eyes. He could see it, he could perceive it. It was there. Perhaps he had been wrong before. It was an odd baby, admittedly, its motions jerky, but perhaps that was not the baby but he himself, shreds of denial. It was his perception that was flawed. He could see and hear the child; what point was there in trying to claim it did not exist? He could think such thoughts around his wife, around the home, but then he stepped out the door, drove to the office, sat in a cubicle with others chattering and muttering around him. There, he didn't know what to believe.

His child, he realized, had never been out of the house. He bought a pup tent and two fishing rods, threatened to take the boy fishing. His wife would not allow it. *Too young,* she said. He tried to take the child with him to the grocery store, but his wife stopped that as well. When he put on a baseball glove and took a ball into the yard, the child stood in the doorway but would go no further. He could see his wife standing behind it, arms crossed. Rudy tossed the ball back and forth against the side of the house, pocking the wood.

Once, trying to force the two lives together, he invited two coworkers home: the dumpy woman and a brown-haired sales-man who often told jokes, chin resting on the top of his cubicle's wall. His wife met them at the door, barred their way. "The baby's ill," she whispered. "Contagious." Rudy took them instead to a bar a few blocks distant, paid for a few drinks, sent them on their way.

III.

The final photographs, the ones he found most disturbing and pondered the longest, were a series of nine images, all exterior, bright sunlight. There was a lake, the light bright off it. There was a picnic basket sitting atop a blanket. There were clumps of his coworkers brandishing cans of beer, wearing shorts and polo shirts. A dog nearly catching a Frisbee, a narrow expanse of mud on the edge of the lake, a stand of sickly pines, the blanket and basket again, his supervisor wearing a chef's hat and turning burgers on a grill, a cracked and mud-slathered shoe.

He had arrived at the company picnic late, without his wife, but, for once, with the child. His wife had not wanted him to go and when he insisted on going forbade him to take the child. It was dangerous, she said; the child might drown, there were mosquitos, the child was not used to the sun. People were demanding to see the child, he said. He had to bring him. No, she said, impossible. Why? he asked, and she gave the same reasons, and he asked again why. It went on for several hours, the child standing there for the whole of it, staring and hardly moving.

For accuracy's sake, he thought, leafing through those last pages, there should be a picture of the closet he had pushed his wife into, a picture of the plain wood door, the key turned to engage the lock. While she battered against the inside of the door with her fists, he had gathered the blanket and picnic basket, filling the latter with things taken hurriedly from pantry and fridge. Taking the child's hand, he left.

He thought at first that the child had released his hand at the door. In looking back he could see the child in the doorframe, grown pale and thin of flesh, but there, looking down, was the child beside him as well, equally ephemeral. He kept walking toward the car though he could not feel the hand, glancing down from time to time to see the child still there.

As they drove, nearing the lake, Rudy spoke to the child, almost frantically, about the lake and the picnic and what fun they would have. The child looked neither at him nor out the window, stared at the glove box latch. When they reached the lake the boy struck him as little more than a flux in the air, a disturbance difficult to perceive. It's me, he told himself. There's nothing wrong with the child, just with me. *There'll be swimming*, Rudy told it. *I don't have a swimming suit for you but it's all right, no one will mind.*

He stopped the car under shade, took the blanket and the picnic basket out of the trunk, opened the passenger door.

He greeted his supervisor, members of his development team. He forced a smile. He saw the woman from accounting in another group not far off, consciously ambled in the other direction. But it was too late. He could hear her calling his name as he walked the other way. Finally, he stopped, turned.

"Rudy," she said. "You came."

"Of course," he said.

"Did you bring your baby?" she asked, straight to the point.

"Of course," he said, and pushed his child out in front of him. The child took one step forward, collapsed at his feet.

"Well," the woman said. "Where is he? It's a he, no?"

"Here," he said.

She laughed, oddly. "You already said you brought him. Where here? With your wife?"

He crouched down, picked the child up, set it back on its feet, watching her eyes as he did so.

"What is it?" she asked. "Are you doing mime?"

"The child's around here somewhere," he finally said. She continued to stare. "He must be with his mother," he offered.

Setting up the blanket, he put out the lunch. The child was still there, hardly visible, its eyes moving jerkily. He put food in front of it. The child did not react.

He sat on the blanket. From time to time someone would notice him, come over to chat briefly, too enthusiastically. They left quickly, without addressing the child.

He tried to stare the child into tangibility but it remained, flickering and static, in a kind of stuttered and half-seen existence. He tried to imagine his coworkers out of existence, narrowing his eyes until they blurred, but when he opened his eyes again, they were substantial as ever.

He looked at the child, helpless and languid. He reached out and poked it, watched it list to one side. There was nothing to the child, he told himself. It was a figment, an infection of his wife's which he, somehow, had contracted as well. Yet, even when he phrased it as directly as that, the child did not disappear. He tried again to move the other direction. He told himself the child was there, present, and it was he who was deluded. He willed the child to swell into full existence, grow ruddy, run about. But the child remained as it was, a creature mostly of air and shadow, present yet not present.

He called his supervisor over.

"Tell me," he said. "On this blanket, what do you see?"

"Raymond," the supervisor said, smiling and tucking his spatula under one arm and tightening his apron, "is this some sort of game?"

"No," said Rudy. "This is important."

"Don't toy with me," he said. "Toy with me and I'll write you up."

"Of course," said Rudy. "Please."

The supervisor sighed. "I see you," he said. He squinted, stared at the child. "I see a picnic blanket. Some food. I see a blanket."

"That's all?"

"That does it," said the supervisor.

"Nobody else?"

"Are you ill?" the supervisor asked.

But still, even after the supervisor had left, Rudy could not will the child away.

He stayed until the others had left and the lakeside was all but deserted. The sun had sunk low in the sky. The child had become slightly less defined, its edges grown blurred, but it was still there.

He packed the picnic things, folded the blanket. He took them to the car, came back for the child. Yet, when he had the child in his arms he walked not toward the car but toward the lake. His heart beat furiously. Kicking his shoes off, he left them in the mud, entered the water in his thin dress socks. He waded in until the water lapped his hips.

Bending down, he let the child slip from his arms. He watched it kick a few times, then breathe in water, its face contorting, features reacting at last. It was awful to watch. Then the face sunk deeper, a pale fishbelly in the muddy water. He was tempted to reach out for it. And then it sunk deeper still and was gone.

He took off his wet pants in the carport. Wringing them out, he put them on top of the garbage cans.

His wife was at the sink, washing dishes. The closet door, he saw, had been kicked off its hingework, had fallen to block the hall.

"How was the picnic, darling?" she asked, voice bright.

"He's dead," he said.

She turned to face him. "Who died?" she asked.

"The boy," he said. "Drowned."

"Whose boy?"

"Ours."

"Our son?" she said. "Little Rudy? Don't be ridiculous—he's been here with me all afternoon."

"I killed him," he said. "I carried him out and drowned him."

"Don't even joke about that," she said. And then, calling: "Rudy? Little Rudy?"

She smiled wide, bent down to pat empty air.

"You see?" she said. "Here he is. Safe and sound."

But he couldn't see, not at all. The child wasn't there, was dead, if it had existed at all. He waited that day and the next and into the next but still there was no child that revealed itself to him, and at last he said so.

She looked him over with slitted eyes. "There's something wrong with you," she said.

"Maybe," he said.

"You can see him," she said. "Right here," she said, pointing to the empty couch. "There he is."

"He's not there," he said.

"Goddamn you to hell," she said. "Little Rudy?" she called. "Come in here and give your father a hug."

He stood idly, his hands loose at his sides. He even squatted down when his wife cued him. He stayed squatted a dozen seconds, until he could feel the blood pulse in his knees, then he stood up.

She was looking at him, her face grown dark.

"No," he said. "There's nothing there."

She turned and stood leaning against the sink, her arms straight so that the skin at her elbows bunched. Her back shivered. He watched her elbows, not saying a thing.

And then her back stopped shivering and she wiped her face. She turned to look at him.

"What?" he said.

He tried to keep his eyes on her but could not. He looked all about the room, saw nothing.

"Get out," she said. "Leave."

Leave, she had said, and he left the house. For a brief moment there was utter elation, and then he didn't know what he felt. He walked the neighborhood slowly, methodically examining the state of his neighbors' fences. The retarded girl was on her porch again, watering the screen door with a hose. The houses, he saw, looked nearly exactly alike. He would pass a house and then, coming abreast the next one, would feel he had not passed the first house at all. Everything was moving too slowly, himself included.

He walked up to Center, sat on a bus bench. He stayed watching the cars pass, the traffic coming in spurts. Down the street he could see the red neon of the motel's sign. He could stay there, he thought. He looked at it a while longer, then got up to go toward it, but instead turned, went home.

He came in, went into the kitchen. It was empty. He went into the bedroom, empty as well. When he opened the closets, he saw only rows of empty hangers. Beside the bed was an envelope addressed to him. He opened his mouth, closed it. He picked up the envelope, tore it crosswise, dropped the halves into the trash.

He closed the album, held it in his lap as he looked about the room. He hoped to see his son again, static before him, or the floor coated with repetitions of his son's face. He hoped for something dramatic and significant. He wanted to be haunted. But even when he squinted there was nothing.

He went into the bathroom, filled the tub with water, stared, tried to make out the swirl of his son's hair as he sank. There was only water, a ripple of shadow through it.

He wandered like that, through the house, all through that night and into the next, seeing nothing, wandering as if he were the ghost and there had never been anyone to haunt him save for he himself. And then he took out the album and turned through it again, hoping to render a new version of his life, one he could bear to live.

Stockwell

I.

He told again the story of Bates, and then the one about himself—Jansen—and then about Gerhardie. Stacks just sat as always with his chin resting on the head of his cane, listening, sometimes grunting a bit. He told like beads Bates with that leg and rest of him you could put a knife right into and not feel a thing. He told of himself, Jansen, who had crept up to slit a disloyal throat mostly out of curiosity, damn the risk. And he told Gerhardie, goddamn handsome bastard who had done fine, not a flicker of doubt through the whole struggle. The handsome, in Jansen's opinion, tended to be like that. But then two months later the car crash and Gerhardie thrown out, the ground breaking his neck and the asphalt scraping the skin all off an already dead face. *Ayeh*, responded Stacks, his head hiccoughing atop the cane, *Ayeh*. And Jansen told Bates crossing the parking lot

alone late at night and being attacked. The numb bastard walked
three miles home with a knife stuck deep in his back, not feeling
a thing, not even knowing the knife was there until he tried to
shuck his clothes at home and found the shirt wouldn't come
free. Didn't even call the police, Bates, just laid down on the bed
on his stomach and bled to death.

You and me, said Jansen to Stack, *sorry pair, the only ones
still drawing breath*. Jansen always claimed he was still alive
because he had remained curious, because he took anything at
all that life threw at him and worked it back in. Nothing could
touch him. Stack just nodded, as he did to everything. *What
about you, Stack? What was it kept you alive?* Stack just sat there,
his chin on the cane and eyes rheumy, saying nothing at all.
Which perhaps was an answer in its own way.

So Jansen told on, told the fifth and last of them, Stockwell,
who was what you would refer to as a *creeper*, had a way about
him, and then he had died too, like the others, how was it exactly he had died, Stack?

"Never was a Stockwell," said Stack.

Jansen stared and then said, no, there goddamn was a
Stockwell, there were five all told. Jansen, Stack, Gerhardie, Bates,
Stockwell. He could recall them all now plain as day.

"No Stockwell," said Stack.

No Stockwell? But he had been telling Stockwell for years
now. Stack had never said *no Stockwell* up to now.

"Never had to," said Stack finally, lifting his chin from his
cane. He pushed himself off the chair and slowly stood. "Today's
the first time you ever mentioned a Stockwell. Nobody by that
name ever was alive."

II.

Lunch and then dinner, a slow round from cafeteria to bedroom and back, and, between, the slow journey out the door
and to the grounds, around the paths. Stack there on the bench

awaiting him but Jansen passing the traitor by. Stack seemed not to notice. Jansen kept on, right down the garden path. *What about you? What was it kept you alive?* he asked of himself, and knew the reply he always gave, *Curiosity and working it all back in, nothing can touch me,* but it had been more than that: he had Stockwell to thank, he thought, *the creeper.* There was a certain dogged persistence to the man that Jansen had stolen for his own. But here was Stack who never said anything now saying no, there was no Stockwell, just the four of them, no one further. It was not to be believed, he thought. But there, too, in the photograph he kept in the dresser beside his bed, only four of them: Jansen, Stack, Gerhardie, Bates. And in Stack's pictures as well, no sign of Stockwell. Yet Jansen was certain there had been a Stockwell, Stockwell had been there. *What about you, Stockwell?* he wondered, *What was it killed you dead?* Was the answer that Stockwell was dead now because he had never been alive in the first place?

The slow sound of the generator dying down, the light above him slowly fading and then flickering as he marked his book by folding the page back. It was the moment he hated most, that slow vanishing of light. Then the light went out altogether and he hated that even more.

If there was a moon, he would turn his chair windowward and continue reading, stumbling on until he fell asleep in the chair, woke stiff and aching a few hours later, stumbled to his bed. If no moon, as tonight, then lying there for hours, the stories springing into his head again, but more vividly this time. He played their lives out again, thrashing against the sheets. Gerhardie: sliding along the asphalt, perhaps hearing the sound of his skull rubbing the pavement. Bates: lying in bed, dying, sheets growing wet with his own blood.

But where was Stockwell? After Bates, every night until this night, had come Stockwell.

And then Stack: not as he had been when they were all loyal together, but as he was now, chin resting on his cane, listening to stories, nearly wordless himself.

And there he was, he himself, Jansen, first seeing the man he planned to kill and then slowly moving forward. Inches from him now, then directly behind. Knife jabbed through the throat, a strange gurgle as the flesh opened warm over his hand and then air hissing out blood-flecked as the man continued to try to breathe, finally going limp. In bed, he saw himself laying the body down, but doing it poorly so that the body rolled face up and he could not help but see the face.

But tonight there was more. Tonight he saw, above the gash, Stockwell's pale face. Thrashing in bed, he was not certain if the face was there because that was how it had happened—that he had killed some unknown man that he later christened Stockwell so as to work him back in with the alive and loyal—or because there was now merely no other place for Stockwell's face to go.

I will make it to morning, Jansen told himself, staring into the slit throat. Nothing can touch me. I will wake up into light and I will put on clothing. I will go out and make the world over again. I will never sleep again.

Barcode Jesus

Burl, B. Gordon, and I had sat down in B. Gordon's living room for just a moment, just to take a load off, and before we knew it we were hashing through the OK City bombing again. Though, being good Christians, we were aggrieved over the thought of anybody injured or dead or covered with debris or in any sort of discomfort whatever, we all had independently come to the opinion that the bombing was a wake-up call to liberal government to get in line with the will of the people. The end was drawing near. You could tell just from the way the globe of the world in B. Gordon's living room was pincushioned and bristly with signs of the times—wars and rumors of wars, famine and flood, all manner of disaster. You get a few beers in you and then you look at that porcupined globe and it sobers you just to think of all that God-driven death, so you reach for another can.

We had had a few by the time B. Gordon started in complaining about the Soulmobile. He calls it the Soulmobile because it is an old bus with Jesus' face on the side and he employs
it to herd people up on Sunday and to convey them relentlessly
to church. It is also his solitary means of transport, and often he
can be found grousing to God, begging him to stretch forth his
hand and give him a vehicle with style to drive around town
during the week.

He is going to Wal-Mart, he tells us, and he's trying to park
but the Soulmobile is too big to park in a single place or even in
two places and the whole parking lot is stopped up. There is no
place to park the Soulmobile that's not going to leave it jutting
across lanes, so he thinks it over and ends up parking it out on
Virginia. While he's there, damned if he don't get a ticket.

"It's like ticketing Jesus," says B. Gordon. "Whether you do
it to Him or to the righteous vehicle consecrated to Him, it's the
same. I ask you: who would have the nerve to fine the Lord God
of Hosts?"

"I thought all the police in this town were Christian," says
Burl.

"I thought so too," says B. Gordon. "I'd been led to believe
just that."

"So you're saying we got an atheist squirreled away among
the police?" I ask.

"Could be," says B. Gordon. "Could be. But let's not forget,"
he says. "Where'd the problem start? Who tempted the police?"

"Well," I say. "Far as I can see, you tempted the police through
your style of parking."

B. Gordon shakes his head. "You know that ain't it, Leon,"
he says. "That's just the superficial view. Me, I'm but the interme-
diary. The problem is Wal-Mart."

This draws Burl and me back some. You can say what you
want about the police: everybody knows they're controlled by
the government which in turn is just a puppet of the New World
Order, so that even if most police are Christian they're caught up
in a non-Christian conspiracy of apocalyptic proportions. But
Wal-Mart is a different story. You don't talk lightly or poorly

when it's a question of Wal-Mart. Wal-Mart is one of the two biggest things that happened to this town, the OKC bombing being the other, and pretty much everybody is convinced Wal-Mart is first on the list.

"Hey," Burl says. "Lay off, B."

"Now don't misdefine me," says B. Gordon. "I have nothing against the store."

"That ain't what it sounds like," says Burl.

B. Gordon puts on his stern hellfire look. "Burl, we're all brothers, aren't we? Aren't we?"

Burl starts scuffing his feet. When B. Gordon starts talking like this, it means he's already won the argument.

"Aren't we?" B. Gordon says again. When Burl still doesn't answer, he looks up at me. "Hell with it," he says. "We're all brothers," he says absently. "Brothers in Christ Jesus. Do you judge your brother?" He looks to Burl. "I ask, do ye judge him?"

"Shouldn't," says Burl.

"Damn right," says B. Gordon. "Now let me finish before you start blurting and spouting." He reaches from where he's sunk into B. Gordon's secondhand but still perfectly good couch and takes hold of his beer, takes a few sips while we all wait.

"You go to Amish country," he says. "Not that anybody in their right mind would, but theoretical now. All the Wal-Marts in Amish country, they got wagon parking."

"Naw," says Burl.

"I shit you not," says B. Gordon. "So when I got that ticket plastered on my windshield I start asking questions. 'B. Gordon,' says I, 'this isn't Amish country, it's God's country. So shouldn't there be parking for God?'"

When he states it that way, by comparison and all, it makes sense. That's the strength of old B. He manages to look at things and discern the logic that everybody else loses track of. When it's told to us that way, we can't help but see the sense in it.

But in this case, sense alone doesn't quite span the gap.

"But it's Wal-Mart, B.," says Burl.

"They even got a McDonald's inside," I say.

"It's not just any ordinary Wal-Mart," says Burl. "It's a Supra-Wal-Mart. Open 24/7. They got a grocery store and a video rental and a hair salon and even a bank—not just a cash machine but a whole fuck-all bank," says Burl. "They got a tire center and you can get hunting licenses from squirrel to deer and there's an electronics center and a shitload of toads and frilly hats and God knows what else."

"You could live there," I say. I am thinking *toads?*

"They got everything but a goddamn church," says Burl.

"Well, why not?" asks B. Gordon.

Burl, drawn up, looks at B. Gordon. "What?" asks Burl.

"Why don't they have a church? They got every damn thing else." B. Gordon reaches out, pulls both of us in close. "Brothers, I ask you," he asks us. "Has Wal-Mart been saved?"

That's how it gets started. B. Gordon doesn't say he's going to be the one to bring the Lord to Wal-Mart but he doesn't have to say it—we know him too well. We know we got to keep half an eye on him, waiting to see when it'll happen.

It's a quiet week. On Monday Burl and I fill up the truck with tree clippers and look for work for a few hours and even batter on a few doors. Nothing's doing. As Burl says, this town is *treed out* and all we can hope for is to live a few months on welfare and wait for attitudes concerning the trimming of foliage to change. If it gets bad enough, I can fire Burl and he can fire me and then the both of us are legal again for unemployment, more or less.

By noon we are back to B. Gordon's, drinking beer. The next day, Tuesday, we reach B. Gordon's at 11:38 by Burl's watch, on Wednesday at 11 sharp. The rest of the week we don't even bother to pretend to drive around. We just save ourselves a little gas and drive straight to B. Gordon's at nine and set about drinking before B. is even out of the shower. It makes for a tough week, all that serious drinking, and by Saturday we are ready for a break and sleeping in, so Burl and I don't go to B. Gordon's but instead spend half the night discussing the problems of a federal government domination. By Sunday morning we are nigh unto dropping and throw ourselves face-first into bed.

Or at least I do. I can't speak for Burl after he stumbles out
my door. What I can speak for, though, is how it seems like I've
only had my eyes closed about two goddamn seconds when
there's a sound going off and I think it's my alarm and I keep
trying to grope around on the dresser and turn it off while my
face is still pressed into the pillow. It takes me a few to realize
it's not the alarm at all, but a horn.

I stumble my way up and open the door. Light hits me right
in the hangover and I feel sick. Damn if it isn't the Soulmobile,
Jesus' cracked and peeling face smiling on the outside.

"Bout time you were up," says B. Gordon. "Sluggard."

Burl is already aboard, scruffed up and blinking, looking
like something the cat coughed up. I groan. "Hop in," B. Gordon
says. "Start praising Jesus."

On the way to the church we stop at the Wal-Mart. The
parking lot is mostly empty and B. Gordon parks where he damn
well pleases. He tells us to wait. He rushes in and Burl and I do
what we can to get back into sleep. I am nearly there when the
Soulmobile door springs and B. Gordon is in, red-faced and disturbed. He is talking about the Whore of Babylon and her splen-
did finery.

"I didn't ask them for their days," he says. "I only asked
them for God's day."

"What's up, B.?" asks Burl.

But he just starts the Soulmobile and lurches it through the
parking lot, whispering under his breath, *hellfire, hellfire.*

At the Church we handpick seats while B. Gordon goes to
fetch a full batch of the holy. We sit in the back, the far left
corner pew, where B. Gordon doesn't have a clear view of us.
That way we can sleep. Which is in fact what we do, me leaning
against the wall and Burl leaning against my shoulder. When we
wake up the sermon is already up and running, not sputtering
either but in full swing, with B. Gordon getting a slap-rhythm
going on the pulpit with his palms and driving it in with his
Jesuses and *Hellfires.* We half watch, even though we have seen
it countless times before, *Praise God,* and know where it is all

leading: straight to the collection plate. He waits until he has the crowd at its height, then passes the plate around while the blood's still tingling. It's a proven fact that's the best way to get people to turn out their pockets to Jesus.

Sure enough, it's *hellfire, hellfire*, then the plate going about ajingle with money, but it is different too, for once the plate's gone around and come back to him, B. Gordon keeps talking instead of sitting at the piano and letting the closing hymn strike up. He is saying how money is good but what Jesus needs of each of us right now is one of those fishing vests with all the pockets. *What the hell?* I am wondering. Burl, being a catfish trawler of no uncommon repute, stiffens beside me and I can see him drop his head so that B. Gordon won't catch his eye.

Jared Barnes, who works at Jock's Nitch Sporting Goods, and who gets a 30% discount, isn't so lucky. Before he knows what is happening, B. Gordon is beginning to recount an anecdote about adultery, in the abstract at first but then in more detail, and Jared properly senses that it is becoming an anecdote that will in the end concern him and Myla Phipps. So when B. Gordon takes a pause in his recounting and licks his lips and asks again who wants to donate Jesus Christ a fishing vest, Jared Barnes figures his marriage is worth 70% the retail cost of a fishing jacket and he shoots his hand up. Jesus usually gets what he wants.

In the same way, B. Gordon angles himself some free photocopying, some posterboard, two card tables, and (probably this one is for himself, not Jesus) one case of pre-made hamburger patties. When he finally strikes up the closing hymn, everybody breathes again. They are afraid of coming to Church, but they are more afraid of staying away.

On Monday I make the mistake of actually getting a job. I'm not quite sure how it happens. I go in just as lackadaisical as always, knowing they will not hire me, but they do. The only interview question they ask is "Have you accepted Jesus Christ as your Lord and Savior?" When I say yes, I'm given the job.

Worse still, it's a government job. It involves coming out to a different city park every day and picking up litter and throwing it away. On the day I am at each park, I'm supposed to turn on the water sprinklers and leave them on for two hours, then shut them off. Somebody who gets paid more will cut the grass. If there are hoodlums, I am supposed to tell them to behave or I will call the police.

The job keeps me busy. It's not that any part of it is difficult, but it just adds up. I last eight days, which for me is none too bad. The problem is that on the second day, in Couch Park, I turn on the water and then forget to turn it off. It stays on all through the week until on Saturday the Little League fields are pretty thoroughly flooded and then about a hundred uptight parents leave messages on the office machine complaining. To top it, on Thursday I come into Tower Park and there sitting on a picnic table is a group of what I judge to be hoodlums. I go up to them and tell them to behave or I'll call the police. They respond, "Huh?" This is about as far as my instructions take me, I don't know what the hell "huh" means in their private language, probably some new jive form of disrespect, so I make an executive decision and start kicking their asses. Pretty soon the park is hoodlum free. When my boss calls me in on Monday about the flooding, he also tells me that nobody under the age of twelve can be defined as a hoodlum, and that I should never take it upon myself to kick someone's ass while on the state clock. Then he tells me I'm fired.

Which is fine by me. It gives me more time for the important stuff. Besides, a man's got to be a fool to work for the government these days, with the end of the world coming on.

I drive down to B. Gordon's and find the door locked, even though a sign tacked above the door reading *Jesus Always At Home* is still posted. I knock, no answer. I go around to the back door and turn the handle, but it doesn't turn. I can't even slip in to borrow a beer.

I hop into the truck and spend some time cruising the town. I go up 6th and then Main and then Hall of Fame. I go by Burl's but he isn't in either. So I turn down on Perkins.

I'm halfway down Perkins, driving slow and careful, just passing the Wal-Mart, when I look over to see the Soulmobile. It is parked not in the lot but smack on Virginia, which reduces Virginia to about 3/4ths of a lane. One line of traffic is going straight, edging against the ditch, while the other has to take a detour through the Wal-Mart parking lot.

Pulling into the parking lot, I walk into the store. The first thing I see, right next to the carts, is B. Gordon. He's sitting at a card table, wearing the fishing jacket (which now is embroidered *Fishing for Souls* over the pocket), pamphlets spread before him. A sign in violet marker reads *First Jesus Church*. There is a coffee can, *Give Unto the Lord* scrawled on it.

"Leon," he says, when he sees me, and nods.

"B.," I say, and do the same. Then I say, I don't know why, "I went by the house."

"I wasn't there."

"No, you wasn't," I say. "That's why I came here."

"You come to the right place," he says.

"I can see that," I say.

Then we rest awhile, me with my hands in my pockets and both of us looking poker-headed.

"What you doing?" I finally say.

"What does it look like I'm doing?"

"Sitting there."

"That's half of it," he says. "The other half is bringing religion to Wal-Mart."

"They let you do it?"

"Not a question of let," he says. He gestures with his chin. "Burl's at the other doors," he says.

I don't know if he's telling me to go down and check on Burl or not, but since I don't have anything else to say, I walk down. When I go in, I find Burl playing with the coin return slot of the pay telephone, a folded card table next to him.

"Burl," I say.

He looks at me nervously, thrusts his hands into his pockets. "Leon," he says.

"I thought you were supposed to set up shop," I say.

"They shut me down."

"That didn't stop B. Gordon."

"B. Gordon's an ass."

We stand there for a minute and then Burl picks up the table, tucks it under his arm. We walk back to where B. Gordon is—or should say was, because by the time we get there he is being dragged off by some blue-vested Wal-Mart employees. He is not going easy, is cursing Wal-Mart and the federal government and talking about the New World Order, all the stuff we have heard before, except that before Wal-Mart wasn't implicated. He curses them as they carry him and his card table all the way across the parking lot, keeps cursing even once they have dropped him in the gutter.

We wait until the guards are gone and then saunter on over.

"So they kicked you out," says B. Gordon to Burl.

"Something like that," says Burl.

"They're Godless," says B. Gordon. "Don't they see the signs of the times? The country's going to the dogs and Wal-Mart's leading the pack. The conflagration's coming unless we can nudge them back on the religious track."

Burl leans the table against his thigh, scratches under his arm. "But they kicked you out," he says.

B. Gordon looks at Burl, disgusted. "So?" he says. "Did Jesus give up when they kicked him out?"

"Kicked him out of what?" I ask.

"But they didn't have no Wal-Marts back then," says Burl.

"That's right," says B. Gordon, pointing at Burl. "All they had was dust and scrub and other misery and they had to scoop a living out of it, and here we are with all the advantages in life. If Jesus could do it then, we can do it now."

"*What* did Jesus do?" I ask.

"Shut up," says B. Gordon. "Get faithful. Get on your knees and pray for Wal-Mart to open its heart and let Jesus rush in."

Five minutes later the card tables are stowed in the Soulmobile, which already has a ticket on the windshield. B. Gordon tears it up and scatters the pieces and then we have linked arms, B. Gordon in the middle, and are marching back to Wal-Mart. *We shall overcome*, B. Gordon is singing softly through the lot, but as we reach the doors he stops and we let go of one another, each of us slipping in incognito.

B. Gordon goes straight ahead, walking the long aisle along the edge of the grocery department, back towards the rows of milk coolers and the McDonald's. I pass the registers, then curve slightly to the right, through the men's clothing and then, with eyes averted, women's clothing and then, accidentally, the women's underwear, which I swear I do not even look at. I hurry on through to the watches.

When I look over my shoulder, I see Burl right behind me, pretty nearby. He is shadowing me. I try to shake him by going up and down through the baby clothes, but he does not shake.

"Burl," I hiss.

He is grimacing at a pack of diapers, pretending not to hear me.

"Burl," I say, loud.

He puts one finger over his lips.

"Quit following me," I say.

He looks puzzled, a little confused.

"Go on," I say, and raise my fist as if to violence him.

He lurches away, looking back once at the end of the aisle.

I walk my way through the books section, then spend some time regarding teapots. They only have two styles, shiny and not-so-shiny, so it does not take up much time. I wander through Sporting Goods, running my hand along the dimpled curved skins of a row of basketballs, then through the pinking shears and to the large aisle, back toward McDonald's.

When I get there, I find B. Gordon set up at a table, his sign in front of him, the pamphlets out of his fishing jacket and all over his table and the one next to it. There are two Wal-Marters in blue vests standing nearby with their arms crossed. I go over to him.

"They're going to shut you down," I say.

"They don't have no authority here," he says. "This is McDonald's, not Wal-Mart."

"But it's a McDonald's owned by Wal-Mart."

"Look," he says. "It's like the Vatican being in Italy but being its own country. Not that I'd ever compare something in this fine state to the evils of Papacy."

I do not know for certain what Papacy is, but I know better than to ask. It does not matter anyway because as soon as B. Gordon starts setting his signs up the blue vests are on him.

"I'm going to have to ask you to leave," one of the Wal-marters says.

"You can't ask me to leave," B. Gordon says. "I'm pleading the sanctuary of McDonald's."

"Do you want me to call the police?"

B. Gordon just keeps arguing, trying to show them the light. He is still trying when the police drag him away.

I go to unemployment and get balled out by Ralph Jenks of all people for keeping my job only a week. Eight days, I correct him, and tell him, *Judge not.* He keeps acting like he is going to refuse me benefits, keeps shaking the form in my face, which makes me remind him yet again that the federal government has rendered us all foolish in more ways than one and him most of all. That makes him wave the papers around a while more, but in the end he signs.

Later I go to the park office and loiter around in the manager's office until they write me out a check just to get rid of me. I take my eight-day check to *Checks Cashed and Pawn* down on 6th and get it all in cash, then divide it into four pants pockets and squirrel some into the bottom of each boot. I am short of comestibles like eggs and sausage and beer, so I go on over to Wal-Mart and get a cart and start pushing it through the grocery aisle. Somehow I end up with the cart filling up with chewing tobacco and crap like maraschino cherries and I know I've got to cut it out or else by the time I get to the checkout I'll have emptied my pockets and be fishing dollars and cents out of my boots. So I go around putting things back.

I am just looking through cartons of eggs trying to find ones without cracks when I hear someone behind me saying under his breath *JesusJesusJesus* like he is selling drugs. While it's a proven fact you can get high on Jesus, Jesus is definitely not a drug. When I turn, I see that it's B. Gordon. He's wearing the fishing jacket, the pockets stuffed full of pamphlets, a button pinned to the front reading "Jesus is Lord," only "Lord" is mispelled "Lored."

"Got them now," he says.

"What?" I say. "Who?"

"I'm a mobile church," he says. "God always wins in the end."

"You haven't won yet," I say, and gesture. Behind him, at a little distance, pretending not to watch him, are two employees in blue vests.

"I thought of that," he says. He unbuttons the top two buttons of the fishing vest, pulls it quickly open to reveal pale red cylinders duct-taped together around his chest like giant firecrackers.

"That isn't what I think it is," I say.

"Sign of the times," he says. "The conflagration's coming."

He keeps moving, two blue-vests trailing behind him. I head straightaway to the checkout and then abandon my cart there and step outside. Leaning against the cart return, I wait for the explosion. History is in the making. I know it will be the biggest thing this town has ever seen. For months, nobody will talk about anything else. All over the country, people will be pushing . more pins into their globes and maps, drinking more beer, shivering with the realization that B. Gordon has pushed us one step closer to the final end.

One Over Twelve

In the middle of January, under the influence of a variety of legal and illegal substances (not the least of these being heroin) which had collectively reduced my red blood count to about 1/12th of what was usual to humans, I had managed to reach a state where I could think clearly again. I thought, over and over again, *Where I'm at in my head is the head of a person about to die*. This time, I could bring myself to believe it enough that not only was my chronic and ultimately inescapable anxiety held in check, but it evaporated altogether. Not only was it possible to write again, but I knew that as long as the proper chemicals held out I would not only write but do the best writing I had ever done.

I could still, I found, hold a pen and make it wander along the paper in letters, despite my having somehow managed somewhere to peel all my fingernails back and away. When I wrote I had to watch my hand carefully and prevent it from pressing the pen too hard, otherwise the damp and empurpled flesh where my fingernails were supposed to be would split and ooze and even bleed. I did not mind it, being hardly able to feel it anymore, only it was difficult afterwards to read what I had written with the blood and ink all mixing together and each trying to outdo the other. Besides, I knew I did not have so much spare blood in me anymore and I could hardly feel a pulse. Where I was at, not only in my head but my body too, was the head and body of a person about to die, or maybe already dead.

In seeing if I could still write with a pen I had scribbled over most of my only piece of paper, even tearing it in some places. Yet I was eager to work. I tried to think where there might be sheets of paper that were still mostly unworded. My eyes, under a careful chemical tutelage, had become powerful enough to bring into the room things that were not in the room and keep them there. I kept looking around for paper and after a while I could see something like paper across from me, on the far side of the room. I tried to get myself to stand up and go over near it, only at first my legs wouldn't move in concert and when one was trying to straighten the other was curling up and thinking. There was only enough blood in me to operate a single leg at a time I began to believe, but then, by a sort of tremendous upswelling of will that without chemicals tightening my veins would have been impossible, I made both legs move at once. I could not exactly think while I was moving them and thus recall nothing until I found myself standing on the other side of the room swaying a little but all right, all right.

I could see now that what I had thought was paper was in fact paper, and I was preparing to claim it when I noticed on the floor beside it a needled syringe which I could not remember putting there, since when I am not anxious I am usually rather meticulous about such things. It was wrong to leave a needled syringe on the floor like that, I thought, and what I wanted to do was pick it up and put it where it would be useful.

Before, when I had more blood and was suffering under my chronic and inescapable anxiety, I would not have had the power to bring myself to pick the syringe up. I used to let the things in the house build up in insufferable ways because I did not know what to deal with first until everything was more and more out of place and disturbing, my anxiety finally fevering to the point where I was forced to be hospitalized. Now, however, I was much healthier and could afford simply not to care about most things, and then the few things I did worry about I could take care of.

By now I seemed to have the syringe in my hand and was on my way back to the couch to put it on the third cushion beside the rest of the apparatuses I used to clear my thought. But then I noticed the syringe was full of something. Not heroin exactly, though there was certainly that in it as well. *If my thought is clear now,* I began to think, *it will only become clearer if I allow myself more of what cleared it in the first place.*

I stumbled down and bound the arm up and pushed the needle about until it struck. After the first push, I could feel thought grown hot in my veins again and death speaking directly to me and through me, its dark colors spilling through my mind to be slotted into the reasoning bone in patterns only I knew how to interpret and put to paper. Only the paper to put them on was on the far side of the room, further away now than it had been before, and I could no longer find the pen either.

Perhaps hours were nodding by. I could see, where the needle had gone in, a bubble of blood on the surface of my arm. I began to think blood would write as well as ink and maybe better, so I dipped my finger in it and used it to write down my arm. I kept squeezing the arm to get more blood and when it wouldn't come much anymore I squeezed my fingertips until my undernail flesh cracked and began to weep.

I closed my eyes and listened to the colors spreading along the inner wall of my skull, my hands running bleeding over my body and translating my skin into language. I kept it up until I was out of breath, then I stopped. My hands fell idle. I began to think, kept on thinking until I was too lost to do even that.

When I opened my eyes, it was maybe early morning because there was light enough to see by. I could not be sure if the light was coming from within the house or outside it, because I had stopped seeing things like that anymore so as to see other things. I could see the couch a long way behind me but it took me some time to figure out that I was no longer sitting on it but instead was in the bathroom and standing in front of the mirror with no memory of getting there.

In a little while I could see my image start to form in the mirror, narrow and thin, my mind and body too, nothing about me in excess. Blood on my skin was forming itself into scratches and words but what interested me was not that so much as what was underneath. If I looked long at myself I could see not only my ribs but all my bones, my flesh hovering and quivering over them like a piece of wax paper so that I could start to see right through myself and see each of my organs atrophied and gone. I could see that there was no blood left in me, only substances I myself had introduced, and these were filling all the empty parts of my body and serving in the place of my lungs, my heart, etc. I opened my mouth and saw all my teeth gone or ground down, though I could not remember this happening either, but it was better they were gone because I was no longer a creature who ate so there was no use for them anymore. My lips too were coated and crusted over pale so that it was hard to tell them apart from my skin. One side of my face, too, had a line of blood running down it and, looking at it, I began to think that that was where my face could hinge off and come away to leave me faceless and gone. If I looked at it long enough, I could almost see my face opening.

I came conscious a while after that. I don't know about the time it was, but there was still light from somewhere and in it I could see blood all over my hands. I could feel blood on my face too, though I couldn't fathom whose blood it was since I had lost all my blood long ago. I could see out of one eye but the other eye was gouged out and gone. The socket was a hole to look into in the mirror, and looking into it I found cached in its darkness a whole flood of new language, and me with no blood to record it at all.

I knew I needed a needle in my arm because I was starting to lose track of what was in the hole and feel things again, and one of the things I was feeling was what was left of my eye spread like a paste over my cheek. By the time I had found the couch again I was already shaking. I could feel my chronic depression surging back so much I could barely manage to affix tube to needle. I had to keep sticking the needle into my arm until by accident I struck the vein and pushed the drug in.

In only a few seconds everything was clear to me and I was in control of my body, my mind. I am not like most people who drugs ruin. Drugs don't ruin me at all—the only time I was ruined was when I was clean. When I was clean, I was so messed up and anxious I couldn't move. Every ten minutes somebody was checking me into the hospital. But the way I was now I was seeing everything and understanding it too.

I could see my death unfurled before me, and all the words that I would find on the path there. If I could have gotten up I would have tried to locate a pencil and paper and started to write my death down. But as it was, I was satisfied sitting there and watching the words scroll out with such brightness that when I opened my eyes, my good eye anyway, it was as if they were burning the words into the walls.

I kept on burning words into the walls with my eye, writing until I could feel my body gone solid again beneath me. I reached over to the third cushion for a full syringe and found nothing but empty syringes.

I looked around the room. There was nothing anywhere that I could see. I just stayed feeling the depression start to ooze back, me trying to suppress it by force of will. I stayed there, trying to remember what it was like to burn words into the wall and thinking, *This time I will really die.*

When my body started to ache I spent a lot of time stumbling around looking for something to inject even though I already knew there was nothing. I spent some time shaking and doubled over, my body in fits from expecting the needle. But I didn't have anything to shoot unless it was air, which probably would kill me. If I had been shaking less and hadn't been so anxious, probably I would have shot air.

I started shouting for someone to come and bring me something that would fit down a needle, only it wasn't a shout so much as a groan or even a whisper. I kept that up for awhile and then turned to thought. I started thinking about a friend of mine who had introduced me to most of what I'd injected into my body. He had never let me down before, I was thinking.

I found myself standing near the telephone table. A few minutes later I came conscious on the floor with the telephone cord wrapped around my legs so that I couldn't even lift the receiver to my face. I tried to get my legs free but they wouldn't come free at first, so I tried to dial the telephone number with my feet. This did not work so well either, the dial tone fleeing to give way to a sort of alarm siren, my toes no longer enough a part of my body to take instruction from my head. While I was trying to press the numbers I realized that not only could I not remember my friend's telephone number, I could not remember his name.

I spent some time lying on the floor, my body farther and farther lost in all the wrong ways, my chronic anxiety making it so it was all I could manage in the course of three or four hours to untangle the telephone cord from around me and crawl away. I thought, *Where I'm at in my head is the head of a person long since dead*, but it did not work so well to say that now that the syringes were all empty. Death's colors were fleeing my head and I could no longer find the places on the walls where I had burnt the words in by sheer force of my vision. I was thinking, *I need to find a piece of paper*, but the house was changing so that nothing was familiar. I could not even begin to see where I might look. I began to think I was going to die without writing my finest work. But what could I do about it, since the house was not even the same house anymore?

I pulled the telephone along the floor and tried to use it again but could not figure out the mechanisms. What I found and was pushing at I wasn't even certain was a telephone. What I needed, I knew, was to get out of the house and find someone who would inject me anew and keep me from dying long enough that I could finish, or rather start, my finest work. I began to crawl about but things kept coming in my way and even if I turned around and went another way the same things would keep on coming in my path. They would come from the side of my missing eye, too, so I couldn't see them. I got up and kept stumbling down, but I was moving forward anyway and eventually touched a wall. My good eye, too, was going dim for no particular reason, but I thought all I would have to do is follow the wall and that would lead me to the door and out of the house. I started around but there were no openings in the wall that I could tell and the wall just kept circling around with me following it. I closed my eye and when I opened it again I could see myself on my knees in another portion of the house, the floor littered with torn paper and trash of all varieties. By the time I had begun to look around, my vision was already beginning to dissolve and had soon faded altogether. I closed my eye and when I opened it again found myself in a long, bright hallway which I thought was God's hallway until my vision began to fade and I realized that it was not a hallway at all but that I had fallen into the empty bathtub.

I lay there, resting. I could see in waves, through the bathroom door, what seemed to me my own house. At least if I forced myself to believe it was my own house it would start to make itself mostly over in that fashion. I lay arranging the space around me with my eye as best I could, my eye snuffed in and out of vision but the world mostly remaining in place. I was shivering in the bathtub though I did not feel cold, and I remained there with my eyes just above the lip, staring out and trying to imagine myself elsewhere—on the couch, going out the door, writing—but such imaginings were too much for me. All I could do was lie there and wish I were dead or, in my more lucid moments, that I had a pen so I could record for posterity what I was feeling.

I began to think that with a little effort maybe I could get death itself to serve as a drug for me and I could use it as a sort of template for everything that was still wandering my head, though not so actively as before.

I uttered a sort of invocation for death to inspire me and, squeezing the tips of my fingers until they began to ooze again,

began to write along the white porcelain. The colors were beginning to open up again, my bursts of vision, and consciousness growing shorter, and I was beginning to think that I did not
need chemicals, that death itself was enough and would serve in
their stead. I had traced two maybe three letters when there
seemed to come a lethargy over me and my hand would not
move anymore. It just stayed against the wall for a while and
then slid down. When I opened my eye, I saw four guttering
streaks of blood, slowly fading. I tried to lift the hand again, tried
to climb from the tub, but could not even move.

I lay there for days, my good eye half open but well given
over. There were no lights, only collapse slow and simple, and
me slipping into it comfortably and with some satisfaction until
men came to pluck me free of it. Men carried me back to save
me, and washed my blood off my body and off the walls. All I
had written was lost and there was nothing left for me to do
except to heal and become alive enough that they would release
me. And then I could go home and gather my things around me
and start again, under the influence of various legal and illegal
drugs, to get back to being 1/12th alive and 11/12ths dead, writing every detail, all for the sake of others. I could imagine it
already, my blood going and my thought clearing, death spreading dark along my reasoning bone and gathering for me into a
dark flurry of language, language being the only thing worth
living, or dying, over. *This time,* I would promise myself, *this
time I will really die.*

House Rules

The first of the house rules, the only one Horst ever manages to recall, is *No leaving the house*. He only remembers because it is posted on both front door and back. Though he can no longer read, that portion of his brain concerned with reading having been *compromised* (Hatcher's language), Horst recognizes the signs. Rarely, however, does their significance strike him until after he has tried the handle of the door in question, found it locked.

Hatcher keeps track of the house rules, and Horst has been instructed to approach him before acting, to inquire if his anticipated mode of behavior will violate said rules. Hatcher has shown him the piece of paper with this instruction inscribed upon it—or rather he has shown Horst a piece of paper with words on it which Horst cannot read. This instruction is not a house rule, Horst dimly realizes, for Thurm, the only other resident, is not compelled to consult Hatcher. Thurm consults no one. Hatcher refers to it as a "Horst-rule." Horst does not understand what he means.

The ground floor has only a few rooms: the kitchen, the common room (staircase off limits), the bathroom, three bedrooms. The bedrooms can be bolted separately from either inside or outside. If they are bolted from one side, they cannot be opened from the other. Each bedroom contains a bed. There is a door in the back of each small room, without knob or handle. Perhaps it is not a door but merely a panel. Neither Horst nor Hatcher has ever seen these ersatz doors open.

Besides beds, there is nothing else in the bedrooms. None of the residents have any possessions of their own. Even their clothing is not considered their own. Each morning they awake to find a neatly folded pile of clothing at the foot of their beds, in place of the pile they left on the floor before falling asleep. If they choose to fall asleep clothed, they awake in the morning naked.

The second house rule involves the distribution of food. *The kitchen is only to be entered once per day, in the morning, to retrieve the day's food.*

Hatcher paraphrases the rule to Horst as follows: *The swinging door is not a plaything. It is a baffle between the kitchen and the remainder of the house. There is no need to enter the kitchen except for food. Food for the day will be found on the table each morning. That food is to be taken out of the kitchen and shared by all three residents of the house. There is no reason to enter the kitchen later in the day.*

On most days, Horst will seem to listen to Hatcher's elucidation of the rule, sometimes even nodding, but moments later he will walk in and out of the kitchen door repeatedly. Sometimes he walks in and turns to go out so quickly that he is struck by the door as it swings back into place. This upsets him. He cannot figure out what has struck him.

Once, Horst managed to wedge his finger in the gap existing between the spindle the door swivels on and the wall. Hatcher refused to help free him. Horst bellowed until Thurm came to his aid.

"The rules are for your own good," Hatcher suggested while Thurm wrapped Horst's crushed finger in a piece of cloth torn from his shirttail.

A Horst-rule related to this house rule: *No eating all the food.* Horst has been found twice, in early morning, sitting on the floor with open boxes and packets of food surrounding him, his face and chest smeared with jam, dry oatmeal scattered about. Hatcher has taken to locking Horst in his room at night. He and Thurm have learned to ignore the sound of Horst's hands beating on the door as they themselves try to fall asleep.

There are windows in the house, six in all—four in the common room, two in the kitchen. The windows are heavily draped. When these drapes are held aside it becomes clear that the windows are boarded over from the outside. The glass of each window is intact. At certain times of the day, light shines through the chinks in the boards, but there is not enough of a gap to allow the residents to see through to the outside.

Horst forgets the windows are there. He shows interest in them only when Thurm holds the drapes aside, and then his interest falls largely on the way he is reflected in the glass. He keeps reaching out to touch his reflection, then back to touch his own face.

The third house rule, the third and last of the original rules Horst and Thurm and Hatcher found awaiting them when, on the first day, they awoke in the house, is *No one shall pass beyond the velvet cord and climb the stairs.*

It is rather difficult if not impossible to move one's body through a locked door, Thurm says, easier to push through a swinging door, easier still to simply step over or crawl under or unhook a velvet cord. Each new rule, Thurm claims, acknowledges more free will in those subjected to it. Each rule is easier to violate than the rule before.

The punishment for violating the house rules varies according to rule, perhaps according to individual as well. The latter assertion is uncertain, for the only individual who has ever been caught violating any of the house rules is Horst. He tries to go out the door until he recognizes the rule on the door. He goes in and out of the kitchen. He extends his hand past the velvet cord, though he has never tried to climb the stairs. Perhaps he does not know what stairs are. And caught, perhaps, is the wrong word, for Horst has never been punished by those who control the house, only by Hatcher.

Hatcher punishes Horst sometimes by striking him with his fist, sometimes by locking him in his room, sometimes by pushing him down and sitting atop him until he begins to squeal. At times, Hatcher punishes Horst even when he hasn't broken a rule.

In any case, this meting out of punishment has no effect on Horst's behavior. It is not corrective. *Compromised*, Horst remains always blissfully unaware. He never changes. He breaks the same rules day after day.

The house is divided into upper house and lower house, the winding staircase in the common room leading from one portion to the other. The velvet rope of the third house rule cordons the staircase off at the bottom. Perhaps there is another rope at the top as well, for certainly those in upper house—if there are residents in the upper house—have never descended the stairs into lower house.

There is a certain degree of curiosity about the upper house. Hatcher wonders if the floor plan of the upper house is identical to that of the lower house. Thurm hopes there are perhaps individuals upstairs who can explain why he is in the house.

Horst has no curiosity about the upper house. For Horst, the velvet rope is something he can rub his face along. He doesn't seem to know what stairs are for, has made no attempt to climb them. Perhaps the portion of his brain concerned with stairs has been *compromised*. Perhaps it is the same portion of the brain as that concerned with reading.

Thurm and Hatcher discuss who controls the house. They speculate about who the controllers are, why they maintain the house, why the three residents have been installed there. They speak of earlier lives, the time before the house, though they speak less in actual memories—which are strangely absent—than of a postulated past. As they speak, Horst rushes about, shuttling back and forth through the kitchen's swinging door. He approaches the velvet rope blocking the stairway, rubs his face along it, rushes back to the kitchen.

These discussions come to a halt when Hatcher finds on a stiff piece of paper two additional houses rules:

1) Do not consider who controls the house.

2) Do not imagine a life before the house.

In his more lucid, perhaps also more anxious, moments, Thurm broods his way along the same logical chain.

"Hatcher is here," he says. "I am here. Why?"

He looks at Hatcher, but Hatcher rarely bothers to respond. He simply stares back at him, face dumb, until Thurm's eyes flick up, fix on the staircase behind them.

"Horst is here," Thurm says. "We know," he says, nodding at Hatcher, "that Horst's brain has been compromised. Can we assume that Horst is here *because* his brain has been compromised?"

"We can assume nothing," says Hatcher.

"Assuming we can," Thurm says, raising his voice, "and I see no convincing evidence to the contrary, then it follows that the others of us are here because we are similarly compromised."

"It does not follow," says Hatcher.

Thurm blinks. "We must ask ourselves," he says, "what is wrong with us?"

The new house rule, a card left with the food in the morning:

Do not speculate on what is wrong with you.

There is some nervous half-speculation on Thurm's part about the new house rule, in particular about the fact that it is written on slick white paper rather than on the textured cardstock of the other rules. Thurm goes so far as to compare the handwriting of this rule with that of the other rules. The handwriting seems to him different, but he cannot be sure. Still, he accuses Hatcher of writing the card.

"We none of us have paper or anything to write with," claims Hatcher, but then refuses to submit when Thurm demands to search his person.

The upper house is the upper house, the lower the lower. It is possible, while still technically obeying the house rule concerning the velvet cord and the stairs, to grasp the banister and lean over the rope far enough that looking up one can glimpse the end of the stairs, the beginning of the upper house. From such vantage, there appears to be a sort of balcony, perhaps a landing. The residents can see the rail that edges it, a small rectangle of ceiling above it, little more.

"Perhaps it is wrong to call them house rules," Thurm suggests, "since we only know that they are applicable to the lower house."

This statement Hatcher takes as a challenge.

All is not well in the house.

At least in the lower house.

Horst rattles the knob of the front door, then that of the back door, front door then back, over and over until Hatcher drags him off to his bedroom, locks him in. He returns to lean with Thurm over the rope, each taking turns looking up until their necks grow sore. From the bedroom, they can hear Horst's muffled screams, the sound of his fingers scratching the inside of the door.

The rules of the upper house perhaps include a rule forbidding one from looking down from the balcony, for only rarely, if ever, do they see anyone. There is some debate over this, Thurm having claimed to have seen a figure, fleetingly. Hatcher suggested at the time that it was merely a trick of the light. Thurm grew quickly unsure if he had actually seen anything.

"Perhaps there are people, perhaps not," suggests Hatcher. "If there are, perhaps they are allowed to look over the balcony, perhaps not. Perhaps they are simply not interested in us."

Hatcher's statement, Thurm admits, covers the possibilities. But it does nothing to reduce them.

Are there rules in the upper house? Thurm argues that there are not, that there is a freedom of movement above that he can admire. Hatcher insists that yes, there are always rules. Certainly those who control the house control all of the house, he argues. There are rules in the lower house, ergo rules in the upper house as well.

"If the breaking of rules goes unpunished," suggests Thurm, "are rules still rules?"

"I punish for them," says Hatcher. "I punish Horst."

"Is this a volitional act on your part or is it the fulfillment of the will of those who control the house?"

"The will of those who control the house."

"Can you prove it?"

Hatcher seems disconcerted for a moment. Thurm watches him set his palm against his forehead, pace a circle around the staircase. Thurm moves back and sits on the couch to watch. He remains there until Hatcher stops pacing, smiles.

"I propose an experiment," he says.

The most difficult moment in implementing the experiment lies in explaining to Horst the purpose of stairs. At first Hatcher and Horst attempt to explain verbally, but Horst's compromised brain takes nothing in. Hatcher stands beside the stairs and mimes climbing, but Horst's brain hasn't capacity to connect Hatcher's antics to the stairs themselves. Hatcher takes the cushions off the couches, constructs a series of makeshift steps by layering the cushions, but Horst is only interested in removing the cushions from the couch and then putting them back on again.

Unhooking the velvet cord, Hatcher pushes him onto the lowest step. Horst stands looking at his feet, then attempts to turn around. Hatcher does not allow this. Careful not to stand on the steps himself, Hatcher tugs one of Horst's feet up, places it on the next step. With his shoulder, he pushes Horst's balance to that foot. He drags the other foot up beside it. Stretching, Hatcher pushes him to the next step.

After an afternoon of this, of painful and slight movements up and down the first steps, Horst manages a step on his own, then several. Some part of his brain begins to function again, while other parts perhaps stop. Hatcher and Thurm watch him clamber up near the top of the staircase and then climb down to the bottom. He keeps going up and down, up and down for hours until finally he steps onto the top stair and then steps past it and then disappears.

For a few hours, Hatcher and Thurm sit at the bottom of the stairs, waiting, peering up to see if they can catch sight of Horst. As they sit, they talk of whether Horst will be punished, whether he will come back unscathed or scathed or not at all. Even if he returns unscathed, Hatcher insists, he might be punished at a later time. If he returns scathed that is proof there is punishment. If he returns unscathed there is no guarantee that he will not one day be punished.

Yet there must be a point, Thurm insists, where one can be reasonably sure that no punishment is forthcoming. Perhaps, says Hatcher, but when? For Hatcher, if one breaks the rules punishment is always there, always hanging overhead. The only modes of existence for those who break the rules are *not yet punished* and *in the process of being punished* and *punished*. Better, then, never to break the rules at all.

They eat their evening meal at the foot of the stairs, digging into the boxes and packets. Each eats from a box for a time and then they swap boxes, eat more. They save the packets for last. They carefully set aside Horst's portion, leaving a little pile of open boxes and packets beside the stairs.

"What now?" asks Thurm, once they have finished.

"We keep watch," says Hatcher. "First you then me," he says, then wanders off to bed.

Thurm stays at the bottom of the stairs, yawning, trying to

keep his eyes open. He gets up and beats his ribs with his fist. He paces back and forth, and after more time has passed goes to Hatcher's room, enters.

He shakes Hatcher awake. Hatcher, he notices, is nude, a fresh pile of clothing already at the foot of his bed.

"What is it?" asks Hatcher.

"Your watch," says Thurm.

"Of course," says Hatcher, and rolls over.

Thurm stands by the side of the bed, waits. He has no way of telling how much time passes. Finally, he shakes Hatcher again.

"Get up," he says.

"I'm up," says Hatcher, but makes no move to get out of bed.

Thurm leaves the room and goes to his own, locks himself in.

When he awakes in the morning, Thurm finds for the first time that no new clothing has been left for him. He is still wearing his old clothing. The pattern has been broken. It is the first time anything has been his for more than a day.

When he goes out to the common room he finds only the common room, the stairs leading up. Hatcher is nowhere to be seen.

Carefully, Thurm disengages the velvet cord, puts one foot onto the lowest step. He lifts his other foot, puts it on the step as well. He stays there a long moment, dizzily, looking up, then steps down again.

Should they go after Horst? Thurm wonders for two days. Near the end of the second day he asks Hatcher. But that would be violating the rules themselves, suggests Hatcher, making them subject to punishment, if there is such a thing as punishment. Hatcher is opposed. Neither of them should climb the stairs.

"But in essence," wonders Thurm, "by encouraging Horst to climb the stairs haven't we broken the rules ourselves?"

Hatcher refuses to consider this. This is not the letter of the law. And Thurm, despite everything, despite having climbed one stair, cannot yet imagine climbing all the way to the top. He agrees that they should proceed with the utmost caution. Better to wait.

Hatcher grows listless. He is hardly himself. He had not realized how much of his day had been bound up in reciting the rules for Horst or in interrupting Horst's game with the kitchen door or in pummeling him. He needs Horst. Without Horst, he is less himself. He tries to recite the rules to Thurm, but it is not the same. Thurm has no interest in rules, and in any case can remember the rules on his own. When Hatcher tries to discipline him, Thurm takes umbrage, leaves Hatcher on the floor with a series of bruises spreading slowly across his chest.

Yet Thurm too, Hatcher realizes lying on the floor, offers him something when taken as Thurm rather than remade as Horst. If he lost Thurm as well, he would not merely be less himself. He would be no one at all.

The food left for them dwindles, food no longer being provided for Horst.

This, Hatcher claims, is an indication that Horst is dead.

Or perhaps, Thurm indicates, it is merely an indication that Horst is being provided for in the upper house. There is no guarantee, Thurm argues, that he will not one day return.

Hatcher dreams that he awakens and leaves his room to find, at the foot of the stairs, Horst's body. Horst is dead. The body is perfect and unblemished, except for the scoriation that already existed round the upper portion of its skull, the site of compromise.

Hatcher sits beside the body, wondering what to do with it. Puzzled, he returns to his bedroom.

When he recounts the dream later to Thurm, he tells it differently. *I dreamt I found a body at the bottom of the stairs*, he says. *It was yours. There were bruises all over your chest*. As he tells it he half-expects that the next day in the kitchen he will find a new rule: *No lying about your dreams*.

Thurm just listens and nods. He says nothing.

In the window glass Hatcher examines the ghost of his own face. It is not a face he can bear to be alone with for long.

Sitting at the bottom of the stairs, Hatcher beside him, Thurm begins to brood.

"Hatcher is here," he says. "I am here. Why?"

"Don't," says Hatcher.

Thurm refuses to look at him. "Horst is not here," he says. "Horst was here but is no longer here. Horst has climbed elsewhere. Can we assume that he has gone somewhere better or at least equivalent?"

"We can assume nothing of the kind," says Hatcher.

"Perhaps not," concedes Thurm. "But I ask you: What place could be worse than this?"

But, wonders Hatcher later, who is to say what is meant by better, worse? They know nothing, not a thing. They have perhaps lived in other places before the house, but have no memories, no experiences to compare to the present.

"I want to climb the stairs," says Thurm.

"It's against the rules," says Hatcher.

Thurm stands up, disengages the velvet cord. He puts one foot tentatively onto the first step. He feels lightheaded, dizzy.

"Wait," says Hatcher. "One more day."

"Now," says Thurm. He places his other foot on the step and then stands there, looking up. He begins to lift his foot, raising it toward the next step. His dizziness increases. He sets the foot back down again.

"Put it off a day," says Hatcher, touching him softly on the back. "In a day, I will climb with you."

We will climb the stairs together, Thurm tells himself, coming off the first step, *we will not grow dizzy. We will go into the upper house*, he thinks as he enters his bedroom, closes the door. *Horst will be there or not there, alive or dead. We will either stay in the upper house or we will return to the lower house.*

Thurm sleeps fitfully. When he awakens, he is naked. Only once has he been allowed to keep his clothing for more than a day, certainly in error. He puts on the clothing he finds at the foot of his bed. Perhaps, he thinks, in the upper house he will be allowed to wear the same set of clothing two days in a row.

He opens the door. Or at least would open the door were it not bolted from the outside. He tries the handle again. He pounds on the door, calls out, receives no response. He throws himself against the door. It doesn't even shudder against the weight of his body. He keeps shouting, keeps pounding.

Hatcher stands in the common room, just on the other side of Thurm's door, silent. He stays there throughout the day, at night creeping back to his room. He can still hear, through the walls, Thurm pounding on the door, begging to be let out.

In a few days, Hatcher thinks, Thurm will have grown weak. He will not have the strength to climb the stairs. *There is no leaving Hatcher*, thinks Hatcher. *I will open the door and bring him out, feed him just enough to keep him alive, no more. In this house, he will be Horst and Thurm both. I will always only be Hatcher, only more so than now. He will crawl and I will watch him crawl and I will teach him the rules and how to follow them. He will go in and out the kitchen door. I will punish him. He will learn to accept his lot; he will be satisfied.*

The Prophets

I.

In a holy vision the Lord came to me and told me to buy myself a shovel and employ it in a righteous use, so I went next door and borrowed one off Boyd Laswell and awaited further instruction. I took to pondering and praying, striving to divine what God might have me accomplish by means of a shovel.

I hauled the shovel through my comings and goings, slung upon my shoulders. I did some walking and standing, praying to God to prompt me where to dig, though I didn't even know if digging was for what the shovel was intended.

Boyd Laswell saw me at it one noon and came after me shouting at me to render him back his shovel. I tried to dissuade him with *Leave off: God has confiscated this shovel!* but he knocked me off my feet and took it. He has always been a mere churchgoer, not properly parceled over to the promptings of the spirit as am I.

I had a few deep and easy nights, then the same fitful vision
came awork at me while I tried to give it no heed. A few nights
and it had harrowed me through, though, and I began to think
that if I kept paying the dream no heed I was on a course to hell.
So I got up in the stark of night and scuffed my way down to the
Central Hardware and broke the door window out with a garbage can lid. Would have gone in after a shovel too, but God
showed me the glints of the dog's teeth as he waited to devour
me. So I went home again and in a little while fell asleep.

Woke up an hour later with my mouth dry and sores on my
lips, a vision of the shovel still rutting about my head. So I snuck
over to Boyd Laswell's and snipped a crowbar from the back of
his truck, then pried the lock off his shed door. Now, I'm no
thief—all I took was the shovel. Would have left money for it,
too, but figured it better to let God reward Boyd in his own way.

I kept with my study of God's holy scriptures, kept Boyd's
shovel sharp-edged and skinned of dirt. My mind was sharp too,
God having made it so. Pretty soon I began to fathom that the
scripture I read and the Church I embraced pursued divergent
paths. I had read the scriptures a hundred times but had never
known the truth until then.

Boyd Laswell came over about twice a day, telling me to
give him back his goddamn shovel and to come mend his shed.
I kept telling him I didn't take his shovel and I didn't do nothing
to his shed door, but the devil made him so he wouldn't be
satisfied.

"All that was took was a shovel," he said. "It's you, Verl,
plain as day."

He tried to bluster his way around my house looking for the
shovel, but I wouldn't let him get far. Hit him on the back of the
head with both fists when he wasn't looking, then dragged him
on out again. Most of the time after that we just stood truce on
the porch, Boyd waiting to see if I would let something slip
concerning his shovel and me voicing out the fact of the spirit I
was fast in the process of discovering: the Church's apostasy.
Boyd was given over to regaining his shovel and did not fully

take my words in. Did not ever say a thing, unless the shovel was involved.

Before taking to bed, I would always pray God to let me know what was to be done with the shovel. I likewise prayed in rising, and added to my morning prayer as well for God to make Boyd leave me the hell alone.

"Look," Boyd said after a few weeks. "You can keep the shovel. All I want to know is that you were the one took it."

"I didn't take it, Boyd," I said. "I don't have your shovel."

He just shook his head and went off. If that isn't a prayer answered, I don't know what is.

I started reading, in plus to the scriptures, the History of the Church, the discourses of all the Presidents and Prophets. Didn't take me long to see where the Church had gone wrong. It was so easy to see I couldn't figure why nobody else had fallen sensible to it yet.

The way it was laid out to me, Ezra Taft was the last real President of the Church worth his salt. All the ones since him were liberals, people who the Lord had inflicted upon the Church for its wickedness. Ezra Taft, though, he was a good John Bircher who saw with a clear eye the importance of our Founding Fathers' Constitution, not to mention the evils of the Federal Government. He saw like it was in broad daylight the conspiracy of the New World Order, and to top it off he supported gardening and self-sufficiency. But even he, by the time he was the President, was old and sick enough to be kept incognito and shuttered up by liberals.

What we needed, I figured, was a return to the full-starched prophets of the past, a return to those *originals* who had been the Church's secret formula to success.

Had that on my mind. Was concerned for the welfare of God's Church, for keeping it on the holy track. It took me all day thinking about and praying for the Lord's help for the Church, so I stopped going to my work and spooled myself away inside the house.

I took to sleeping through the day and carrying the shovel around the street at nights, when Boyd was asleep, until the police cruisers took to pulling up alongside me and serving me hell. After that, I took mostly to staying in.

Boyd came by so much that I started letting him off the porch and into the front room. Sometimes he would ask with about one third of a heart after the shovel, but pretty soon he wore himself out on that topic altogether. My former bossman came over a few times and knocked hard enough to rattle the door in its frame, but me and Boyd stayed quiet and pretty soon that one went away for good.

I offered Boyd the fruits of my study. I told him how liberals had seized the reins of the Church, leading the horses to run full bore away from God.

"What we need, Boyd," I said, "is a return to the Prophets of the past."

But Boyd would not admit yea or nay, nor even pay attention. That's how he was.

II.

Then one night, I figured the vision's meaning through and through. I stood up and slung the shovel athwart my shoulder and walked over to knock on Boyd's door. A few minutes of pounding and he came to the door mumble-eyed, his holy underwear in shameless view to all the world. Didn't seem too pleased to see me. But, after all, he didn't know what I was there to see him about.

"My shovel," he said, when he saw me carrying it.

"Get dressed, Boyd," I said. "We're driving to Idaho."

He sat looking through me a long time like I was stupid or something. Shaking his head, he went back inside and closed the door.

I opened the door and invited myself on in. Boyd was back to his bed already. I shook him awake a little.

"Loan me your truck, Boyd," I asked.

"Let me sleep," he groaned.

I asked after his keys, but he wouldn't tell me or didn't know what I wanted. I got on the bed and shook him a little more, but that didn't do anything for him neither.

I looked for his keys on the kitchen counter. There were some hooks on the wall by the back door, but nothing in the way of keys to hang from them. Taking Boyd's trousers from the living room floor, I found the keys in a front pocket. I found his wallet there, in the back pocket, and borrowed a few dollars for gas.

"Boyd," I said. "I'm taking your truck to Idaho."

Boyd didn't say anything, so I took the truck and left.

I drove three hours to Idaho, considering God's words the whole way. Got there an hour before the sunup, the sky threatening light, then drove up and down the town until I stumbled onto the graveyard.

I walked about a bit, the dew clinging to the toes of my boots, until I started to see the honorable Benson name slung all about the headstones. I walked down through them until I found the Prophet Ezra Taft and then set to digging.

Took me about two goddamn seconds to know digging with a shovel was a waste of time. I left the shovel by the headstone and took a thinking walk around the graveyard, trying not to walk on nobody.

Near the back fence I found a digger, the keys in it, just as if God had placed it there for my use, which he had. Climbing in, I started it and threw the gear in. I drove back to Ezra Taft Benson's grave as best as I could manage, clipping down no more than a few headstones. I started in digging, mastering the trade as I went. First thing I almost tipped the bastard over backwards, but then I got it figured and took a few gouges out of the ground, dumping them wherever the scoop had a mind to dump, which was sometimes back in the same hole. Took the hole down until dawn was near breaking and I had scraped and splintered the lid of the casket, then scrambled down on my own to finish off with Boyd's shovel.

When I got the lid up, I could see the old prophet's face perfectly preserved for a moment, privately collapsing as the air struck it. I had to hang my face over the side of the grave a little and breathe, but then I thought maybe this was God's test for me. Getting down there, I pushed at the body a little, seeing if the bones were integumented together sturdy enough. They seemed to be so, so I grabbed him by the shirt and lifted him out.

I shook the bugs out, best I could, then got him all secured under a tarp in the back of Boyd's truck. I got back in myself, drove.

When I pulled the truck back in around lunchtime, Boyd was setting on a lawn chair in the driveway, arms crossed.

"Where you been?"

"Idaho."

"Shit, Verl. You took my truck all the way to Idaho?"

"You told me to," I told him, handing back his keys. "You volunteered it."

He threw his weight around some more, then suddenly calmed down and started sniffing his way around.

"What's that smell?" he asked.

"Nothing," I said.

He went to the back of the truck and looked under the tarp. Went white once he saw the prophet there.

"Jesus," he said. "What is this all about?"

"Don't worry your pretty head none, Boyd," I said. "That's the Prophet. I'm just saving the Church is all."

"You take him back," he said. "Now."

Boyd could be pretty stupid sometimes. "I can't take it back," I said.

He just started whimpering. "Get it out of my truck," he hollered, "before I call the police."

"Sure," I said. "Lend me a hand, Boyd."

He wouldn't help me, though. Just went into the house, and me after a little while following him in.

"Going to look awful funny to the police," I told him. "You

with a body slung in your truck."

"I didn't do nothing," he said.

"Don't matter," I said. "What matters is what it looks like. And what it looks like is awful funny."

I didn't wait for an answer but went back to my own house and clapped the door closed like I was angry or something. Didn't take him long to be coming after me.

"All right," he said. "I'll help you get it out."

I didn't know quite what to do with him so I told Boyd just to lean him against the garage wall and maybe brace him up a little in a corner so he wouldn't turn and yaw over.

I sent Boyd home, then sat there in the garage looking at the fellow. He didn't look like no Prophet, his flesh mortally gone and what was left murling on the bones. I wondered if maybe I had gotten the wrong Benson on my hands instead of Ezra Taft. But no, the stone had read Ezra T. all right.

I tried to stand him up so he would stay on his feet but the body was not exactly cooperating and wanted to stay board-stiff and hands to sides. I leaned him against the wall, then thought it over and stepped next door.

"Got some wire?" I asked Boyd.

"What's to keep me from calling the police, now that he's out of my truck and in your garage?"

"Neighborly spirit," I said.

"By God," he said. "I'll call them."

"Just fetch me the damn wire," I said.

He went out to the shed, me following, and fished out a coil of solid wire. I took the coil and slipped it over my arm.

"I wouldn't call them," I said. "God don't like it."

"God?"

"I'll figure a way to make them think you were in on it, Boyd," I said. "Thanks for the wire."

I spun two turns over the garage rafter and started hooking the wire to the body, but there was no easy place to hook it on. So I went on back to Boyd's.

"Got a drill?" I asked.

He started to turn, then hesitated, darted back my way. "Drill," he said. "I don't even want to know."

Pretty soon I had him wire-slung and standing more or less. I had him looking sleek as he could look in a suit that I borrowed from Boyd's closet while he was asleep.

I decided to see what I could do about making him look a little perkier. I went into the house and got some of the beauty supplies my wife had left a few years back when she had seen fit to leave me so suddenly for no worthwhile or explicable reason. There was some bright neon-red lipstick and some peach-colored powder with a puff and some mascara and then a few other supplies that I didn't even know what part of the body to rub with. Those first three, though, I took out into the garage.

I started with the lipstick because I thought it would be hard to go wrong. You've got the lips, you've got the lipstick, seems pretty simple. Only the problem here was there weren't really no lips to speak of. I had to make do with what little flesh was left and color in on the teeth for the rest. Then I went in and got some tissue like I had seen my wife do, only there wasn't any tissue, only toilet paper. And then I pressed it against the lips, like I had seen her do.

The peach stuff I just kind of powdered all over with until his face looked like he was coated with pollen. The mascara I finally gave over on because I couldn't see the point of making eyes look bigger that weren't even there in the first place.

I went inside and found my spare reading glasses and smeared the lenses with Vaseline. I put them on the Prophet and he looked good enough, better anyway, almost penetrating with the eyeholes gone uncanny through the Vaseline.

I couldn't help but calling Boyd over for a look. He didn't want to come but I kept threatening to turn myself in and take him with me, so finally he shuffled over.

"Jesus Christ!" he said when he saw the Prophet. "You've gone crazy, Verl."

I shook my head. "I'm the only sane one in the bunch."

"You got to get this body out of here," he said.

"Like hell," I said. "This here's the Prophet, come to lead the Church back to the track."

He kept calling me crazy until he was tired out of saying it, but I just stuck to the truth and kept telling him about the dream of the shovel and the steps of how I had gotten from a shovel to having a dead prophet—"The last true prophet!" I told him—in my garage. I used God's logic on him. Boyd just shook his head and looked sad about his life and maybe about my own. Deep down he was a compassionate person, Boyd, even though he was basically as dumb as a post. That was the beauty of him and why I wanted to take him along the path to salvation. Suffer the little children, if you know what I mean.

"I'm going home," he said.

"But Boyd," I asked him, "don't you want to save the Church?"

"You do what you want," he said. "I don't want to hear anything about it."

I followed Boyd back home and before he could shut the door got my foot wedged in.

"It's me, Boyd," I said. "Let me in."

"Like hell," said Boyd.

"Boyd," I said. "All I want is one more thing from you and then I'll leave you alone forever."

He thought that one over awhile, stamping on my toes in the meantime. But when he saw I wasn't going to let off easy, he started to crumble.

"What is it?" he asked.

"Just come tell me how he looks for once."

"I don't need to see him again to tell you he looks like hell."

"Last thing ever," I said.

"Promise?" he asked.

"Promise."

"Jesus, he looks like hell," said Boyd.

"You mean it?"

"I don't know how you did it, but you made him look worse," Boyd said. "What you got to do now is get his sorry ass back into the ground."

"He's going to lead the Church, Boyd."

"Like hell he is," said Boyd.

"I am going to raise him from the dead," I said, which was the truth.

"I'm going home."

"I'm telling you the truth, Boyd," I said. "Don't believe me, and you're destined for hellfire."

He shook his head and walked out.

"I mean it, Boyd!" I called. "God needs you!"

I went to bed but like hell could I sleep. Kept having dreams about the Prophet in my garage. In my dream he was begging me to hurry, and God seconding him.

I got out of bed and made some chicory, me being the sort who because of his religious knowings doesn't drink strong drinks like coffee even though that is what I mainly want to drink all the time. I took my chicory out into the garage and sat on the steps looking at the body. I set the cup down and started turning around the body, circling around it, and thinking. Then once I got around behind it and I felt like I had the holy power coursing through me I put my hands on the head and blessed him to rise up and walk, and be alive.

Then I stepped back. I waited for the Prophet to stand and walk but he did nothing of the kind, just kept hanging there by the wires.

I decided that maybe a body dead and buried and in the ground for as long as that and made up now to look worse than it had in the ground might need some surprise or some kind of jump-start. So I kept on crouching down and hiding behind him, then leaping out yelling, "Rise up and walk! Rise up and walk!" It seemed like a good idea at first but after a few hours the idea didn't seem so good to me anymore, but God knew I had tried so for once he let me get some sleep.

In the morning it was all the same things and me trying to figure out how to get the Prophet onto his feet again so as to show us where the Church went wrong and start it back where it would go right instead.

I thought maybe if I sprayed him down with a hose first that might help matters, but what happened was the hose just spread what was left of his skin all over the garage. I blessed him every five minutes or so to rise up and walk but he was a stubborn bastard and wasn't having none of it. I kept trying to surprise him but he wasn't interested in that either.

Around nightfall, nervous from the dreams about to come my way, I called it quits. I made my way inside to think the problem through with all my fund of logic. But it wasn't the sort of problem that would give over easy to logic. Once that came evident, I got out God's Holy Word, which had never led me wrong before, and opened the pages and looked for wisdom therein:

And God said, Let there be light, and there was light.

Maybe, I thought, this is a message from God directly to me. But I have come to think that it is better not to act until confirmation comes, so I kept flipping my way through all the holy books until after seven or eight fake starts I came onto:

For the Word of the Lord is truth, and whatsoever is truth is light, and whatsoever is light is spirit....

I had read that a hundred times, I guess, but it felt like God had had his prophets put it in there just for me to find at that moment, so I could go about saving the Church.

III.

Boyd had locked the front door, but one of the windows was open a little and the screen popped right off in my hands. He was in bed even though it was only a little past midnight, so I shook him awake. He just about had a coronary, to hear him talk. He wasn't so happy about me showing up, but you could always count on Boyd not to hold a grudge long.

"Still got that generator, Boyd?" I asked once he had calmed down.

"You can't borrow it," he said. "Let me sleep."

I went out of his bedroom and rummaged through the house a little but could not find the generator anywhere. Tried Boyd's garage. Then I took the crowbar out of Boyd's truck again and pried the new door off the shed. It was a little better door than the first one, but didn't make any difference in the long run.

The generator wasn't there, but there were an orange utility cord and two spools of bare wire, and these I took back to my own garage. I worked the wire into one of the cord's positive sockets and then the second wire into the negative socket. The hole for grounding I just left like it was. Then I wound both spools of wire crisscross around the Prophet's body and twisted them together once I ran out of wire.

I plugged the cord in and the first thing it did that I saw was make the Prophet start to hiss and smoke, though he wasn't dry enough to catch flame. Then the wires on him started to glow red and the extension cord was hot enough that the plastic started to melt too. I was going to pull it out but I didn't want burning plastic all over my palms so instead I ran into the house and opened the fuse box and saw that the pennies spanning the gaps were glowing red hot as well.

I ran into the kitchen to find something to pry the pennies free with, but by that time all the sockets in the house were spitting sparks and such, and then from the garage came a big flash and everything went dead.

I took a flashlight out of the pantry and had a look around. Most of the sockets were black with a smell coming out of them. When I opened the fuse box the top penny was melted down over the other pennies and fuses and all of it burst apart or looking none too pretty. I had never seen the like and as I looked at it I started to think it meant something or perhaps was a sign of some sort, perhaps that God liked what I was doing and was telling me to keep it up. And then I began to wonder since all this had happened in the house about what had happened in the garage. But there was no way I was going out there alone.

I went over to Boyd's and stared in his plate glass window. He was sitting in front of the TV in his bathrobe eating popcorn. There was no reason not to disturb him. I rang the doorbell.

"Boyd," I said, when he opened the door. "I got a power outage. Lend me a hand."

He groaned, but then he tightened his cinch and came along, his good-naturedness working on him and kind of blacking out his good sense.

"What you doing up, anyway?" I asked.

"You ought to know," he said. "How do you expect a man to sleep once you climb through his window?"

When he got in and saw the fuse box, he just stared at it.

"What makes you think I can fix that?" he asked.

"I don't know," I said. "You're pretty handy, aren't you?"

He took a screwdriver and undid one of the wall fixtures, showed me the wires all burnt out behind the plug.

"You got a few thousand dollars?" he asked.

"Not precisely," I said.

"You're going to have to rewire the whole house," he said. "What you going to do?"

"God provides," I said.

Boyd shook his head.

"He's always provided before," I said. "Problem with you, Boyd, is you don't give no heed to all the miracles around you."

"I can't do anything about your power outage," he said. "I'm going home to sleep."

"Wait a minute," I said. "Take a gander or two out in the garage."

"I already know who's out there," he said.

"I need to figure out how I went wrong," I said. "I'm afraid of what I'll see."

In the end, I got him curious enough that he came. I went into the garage first, waving the flashlight, he following.

I looked around first at the socket and saw it was shot to hell. The flameproof wall was still smoldering and toxic so I had to stamp the sparks out. The cord too was a hell of a mess. I followed it slowly out, slid the flashlight up the Prophet's body.

He was burnt all over and Boyd's suit burnt off him and the wires I had run around him sunk deep into his body now and probably held up only feebly on the bones. But I'll be goddamned

if his one hand which before had been down at his side wasn't
now raised up above his head.

"See that," I said to Boyd. "His hand?"

"What about it?"

"Will you look at that?" I asked. "There's a miracle if I ever
saw one."

"What?" asked Boyd.

"His hand, his hand!" I said. "He's lifted it up."

Boyd took the flashlight and went over to take a look at it,
then looked at the shoulder joint too.

"The electricity must have done it," he said.

"God did it," I said. "That's his sign to *you*."

Boyd turned around, what I could see of his face in the
afterthrow of the flashbeam contorted and tight.

"You rigged it!" he yelled, his face turning dark.

"Get thee behind me, Boyd," I reasoned. "If you just stop
and think it through a little you'll hear what God is telling you."

But he didn't want to hear nothing. Not Boyd. All he wanted
was to stamp on out and take my flashlight with him.

"Boyd," I yelled after him. "You got to believe! You got to
believe!"

But some people even God's miracles won't touch. Some
people won't even listen to God when he hits them over the
head.

The Progenitor

I.

To please the progenitor, the ground-muscled untether one of the men and fire the extreme of his cord. Observed through a spyglass, the man floats up as descriptions of his ascent are shouted to the progenitor. The ground-muscled record the time and progress of the ascent until the fire reaches the body and the man's helial lobes warm and burst. He burns quickly, falling to ground as a fine sift of ash.

Largely, however, the men remain unmolested. By propelling themselves about with careful motions of the hand, they can progress along the arcs of their tethers. Their tethers are of sufficient length that a man by this means may easily reach the others tethered nearest to him.

When not required, the men may converse or quietly attempt copulation. This is permitted by decree and toleration of the progenitor.

Mornings, certain men may be found enclustered, clinging together in the air until the sun warms them or the ground-muscled below tug their cords and shake them apart. Rarely, they grip one another so tightly that the ground-muscled must haul them down hand over hand and beat them until they fall slack and let each other go.

The attendants examine the arrangement, assuring themselves the rows are straight, the tethers knotted at the prescribed distances along the rails. At sunset, the progenitor outswells the close of his day and the shape of the next in a lilting, struggling tongue.

At a signal from the ground-muscled, the men part their skin and display their helial lobes, stroking the surrounding integument until the lobes begin to glow. They are required to maintain a smooth glow for the duration of the progenitor's outswelling and for a period of reflection thereafter. Those who cannot work the integument into proper glow are immediately untethered and set aflame.

In the early light men can be found awake and pushing themselves open-mouthed through the air, gathering the cold-slowed insects upon their tongues. They eat nothing else and drink not at all, unless it be that they preen dew off their own person.

The more enterprising entrap insects without crushing them, trying to seduce these to nest upon their person. Though this is always difficult, it is not impossible with certain varieties. If a flourishing colony is established on the skin, the time spent gathering food will be greatly reduced. However, difficulties exist. If more than one colony gains hold, a man's buoyancy will be impeded. If the reduction in buoyancy becomes discernible from the ground, the ground-muscled will haul the man down so as to laden and musculate him. In addition, some insects are carnivorous. They burrow into the flesh, eating the bodies imperceptibly from the inside out until all that remains is an empty outer skin, ribbing and ballooning with air.

Those to be ground-muscled are selected by preceptors trained in the art by the progenitor. These preceptors, upon the death of a ground-muscled, walk among the tethers, scrutinizing the men bouyant above their heads, sounding the tension in the cords. A man might be chosen for a slight lack of buoyancy, for having a body structure likely to survive the musculation and ladening, or according to a more obscure, intuitive reasoning.

Once chosen, the man is hauled to the ground. Two of the preceptors are bound to him, one to the left side, the other to the right, and by such means he is prevented from ascent. The man is brought to the ladening place where he is bound to the slab. The flesh of the limbs is slit and pulled back to make way for the insertion of wooden disks and nails and pieces of jewelry between skin and muscle, and then it is sewn down. The body cavity is sawed apart and eviscerated of all but the helial lobes, for without the lobes, the body slowly poisons itself. The lobes, however, are crimped and suctioned, drastically reducing their size. The body cavity is filled with sodden sponge, a length of rope coiled in the place of the colon, and then sewn shut.

The man is released from the ladening slab and, if still living, caused to stand. If his bones shudder and collapse, as is not uncommon, the body is quickly disjointed and fed to the progenitor. If the bones hold, however, the man is taught to walk and is accepted into the weighty, earthbound fold.

Those whose bodies prove most resistant to the ladening, those who become thoroughly ground-muscled, will sometimes be chosen for further descent. They are again cut open, sponge and rope removed and replaced by iron filings and clinks of chain. They are further laden with greased rings slipped over their extremities, their bodies strung in steel and thoroughly exoskeletoned.

They are secured at the end of a chain. Later, they are led by the ground-muscled to the marsh. There, they begin to sink. Before the end of the day, they have vanished entirely.

It is the task of the ground-muscled to hold to the end of the chain, preventing the burdened man at the other end from breaking free and escaping. Though many ground-muscled have been hauled under the earth for refusing to release the chain, there is no instance of the submerged returning of their own accord.

Once in a year, the ground-muscled are called to provoke the progenitor, prodding him and massaging him until he begins to scream and puff. His body is rolled out of the penetralium and edged nearer to the open doorway. Under the touch of sunlight, he begins to expel strings of jellied larvae.

These larvae are caught with hooked staves called *fornii* by the ground-muscled, then smeared against the roof of the dome. They are allowed to develop independently until the fluids dry. At that time, they begin to scutter across the roof first with their tails and then, as these are dropped, the knobs that will develop into limbs.

When the torso is formalized, variegated sufficiently to prevent the slippage of a tether, the larvae are anchored and taken from the dome, sent skyward, left to hang. If they survive four days without a decrease in buoyancy, they are allowed to remain alive.

Upon the death of any man, a lament is sung by those tethered closest to him, reiterated in bolder tones by the ground-muscled below. The body is tugged down and opened, the helial lobes lanced to release a precise measure of their pressure and then resewn and bound in tar. Untied and released, the body floats slowly upward until it reaches a point of equalized pressure and is carried off upon the wind.

The men believe their bodies will float forever. They are supported in their belief by the periodic inflow of bodies on the upper currents of the air, the corpses shuttled about on the wind.

At times, the upper air is absent of bodies entirely. At others, they all flood back and seem clots and lesions spread all along the surface of the sky.

II.

All can be said to go well until the day the progenitor begins to act strangely. In the place of larval strings, he extrudes forth malformed helial sacks which, in bursting, injure and sometimes kill the ground-muscled. He calls not for food but for fistfuls of gravel. His increasing heaviness leaves a fixed impression on the penetralium and the walls of the surrounding dome groan. The ground-muscled hurry to please him but he will not be pleased.

The attendants take shovels and dig in the places where the burdened have slipped beneath the surface of the earth. Most often, the holes fill with water and digging cannot continue. Sometimes, however, the burdened are found dead and tangled in their chains, entrapped in the roots of trees, their throats packed with mud.

Over the course of several days, the progenitor worms his way out of his enclosure and, after many flailing attempts, gains his feet. Soon, he finds his balance. For the first time, he takes a step, his feet sinking deep into the earth.

The ground-muscled bustle about. In his subsequent lurching steps, many are mangled and crushed. He progresses one step at a time, his feet sinking deeper until he wades in earth. The remaining ground-muscled counsel one another and observe him from a distance. The progenitor struggles his way downward, into the ground, until only his head remains, a misshapen pyramid riding on the surface, the ground shuddering as he tries to breathe.

One of the ground-muscled unties a tether from the rail and reties it around the progenitor's neck. The man at the cord's end rises just behind the progenitor's head, almost as if standing on the scalp.

The other ground-muscled rush to untie the other tethers and do the same, until the progenitor's neck is strung thick with cords and the head no longer threatens to slip below the surface.

While they congratulate themselves, they realize the progenitor is dead, strangled. They remove the ropes from his neck, watch the progenitor's head slide down and under the earth, the ground bubbling.

The progenitor's body resurfaces, its planes sharpened, the surface material shined and slick. He looks alive, but he is still strangled, still dead.

Time has ended. The ground-muscled laden the progenitor's body until it sinks again. They crack the dome, destroy the penetralium. They light tether after tether until all the tethers are aflame and released. As they make their way toward marshy ground, the sky is a torment of fire and ash.

The Gravediggers

They scraped clean the ground, their shovel blades fouling in the weeds and tearing them loose. They beat the hard earth underneath until it broke all across its surface and the crust of it rattled and came free. They worked the man's shirt off his shoulders and off his arms and spread it atop the weeds to one side of him. They heaped the shirt with platelets of loosened earth, the weeds beneath pushing up the edges of the shirt where the dirt was not on it.

They rested the blunted shovel blades against the hardpan. Each of them raised a foot to the top rim of the blade and purposed most of their weight down onto the blade. The shovels skittered over the earth and turned away, bringing off a scattering of dust, the blades scraping shiny lines along the ground.

"Goddamn," said Earl.

"Goddamn is right," said Mason. "Let's quit."

"Can't quit," said Earl.

Mason shrugged. He ground the blade of his shovel against the earth and cast his weight upon it. The shovel scuttled forward without biting.

He let the shovel fall.

"Pick it up," said Earl, his palms curved around the ball of the shovel handle, his chin resting atop his hands.

"Maybe I won't," said Mason.

"Maybe you won't," said Earl. "The hell with you."

Mason stooped and took the ball of the handle into his hand. He swung the shovel by its end and let fly with it into the weeds. He squatted down on the rimming of the shallow hole, not deep yet to the finger.

Earl stopped digging. He upturned his shovel and squinted along the blade, the edge of it grown shiny from the hardness of earth.

"Need a pick," said Mason.

"Just what we don't have," said Earl.

"Nothing doing without a pick," said Mason.

"Can't quit," said Earl.

"Hell I can't," said Mason.

"Get up," said Earl, prodding him with the shovel blade. "Get digging."

They set their shovels to the ground. They scraped lines into the dirt and drew away piles of fine sheening dust. The wind was at the pile and swirled the dust around the depression and into their eyes and up their throats.

Mason coughed. He kicked the dust out of the hole and scattered it into the weeds. He set the shovel aside.

He stepped into the hole and spread apart his feet. He unbuttoned the upper flap of his trouser, folded it aside.

"Put that away," said Earl.

Mason shook his head. He urinated, his water splattering off the dry earth of the hole and smearing on his boots. He spread his legs wider. The liquid lay for some time on the surface, soaking in, the dirt staining darker.

He buttoned his flap. He took the shovel and prodded the earth with the blade's tip. He stood on the wings of the shovel and slowly worked the blade through the dirt. He leaned back. He broke free a chunk, shovelled it onto the dead man's shirt.

They worked side by side, shovelling until the hole had grown deep past their ankles and the soaked earth was gone and the shovels again slipped along hardpan.

"Haul yourself out," said Mason.

"Don't need to piss," said Earl.

"Don't matter," said Mason. "Do it anyway."

Earl turned his back to Mason. He unzipped his trousers. He stood braced with his feet wide apart from one another and his hands hidden at the waist.

He looked back over his shoulder.

"Well?" said Mason.

"Nothing in me," said Earl.

"Force something out," said Mason. "A drop or two."

"Haen't nothing to force," said Earl, zipping his trousers and turning.

"Start spitting," said Mason.

They leaned on their shovels, the hair of their hands and arms powdered with dust, the dust running into silty channels with the sweat of their faces. The bottom of the hole had grown shiny and slightly deeper.

"Got the creek," said Mason.

"Haen't no bucket," said Earl.

"Hell, got to have something lying around down there."

"Don't have no time for that," said Earl. "They gone to be coming here, and him still to do up."

"I am gone," said Mason.

"You haen't," said Earl.

"Hell I haen't," said Mason.

He let his shovel fall and started walking. He heard Earl behind him, yelling. He skirted the summit and started down the other side. He turned his head, watched Earl's face sink down and be gone.

He walked the burnt half-mile downhill to the stream. He walked along the bank and found there the cracked sole of a boot, the stitching eaten away. There was string tangled through the bushes and a squirrel or chipmunk strangled up in it and long dead, going to bone. He unraveled the string, pulling it through the squirrel's body. He broke off a length and balled it up and worked it into his pocket.

He walked along the creek in the other direction and there found nothing. He sat down on a rock on the edge of the stream. Shucking off his boots, he slid his hands down the warm throats and prodded the worn padding, fingering the loose stitchwork.

He let one boot fall. He regarded the cracked leather of the other's upper and turned the boot over, rubbing the joint of a thumb across the remains of a sole. Then he put the boot back on his foot. He picked up the other boot and stood to carry it to the edge of the bank. Tipping the boot in, he let it fill of its own accord until river was spuming out the top. He lifted the boot out. He carried it by the pulls to the base of the hill and started up, the water drizzling through the cracks of the upper and the sole. He loped up the hill, his legs and feet growing damp.

He circled the summit and came around the edge to see Earl at the hole, striking at it with the edge of the blade. Earl stopped and watched his brother step down to stand in the hole and there upturn the boot.

A few drops of water dripped out, touched the dirt, and were gone. Mason looked into the boot.

"What good are you?" said Earl.

Mason said, "Give me your boot."

Earl leaned against the shovel. He lifted a foot, showed Mason the bottom of each boot in turn, the soles worn through and the socks beneath grown threadbare and ragged.

"We are in a sorry state," said Mason.

"Not so sorry," said Earl. He pointed to the corpse, its stomach swollen with heat and bloat. Mason left the hole and went to the man. He put his hand on the belly, felt it half-firm. Pushing into it with his knuckles he saw it balloon around his hand so as to swallow it. He opened the button of the man's pants and drove his fist deeper. The belly pushed against the fly, the zipper splitting its teeth.

Mason returned to the hole.

"Your knife," said Mason.

"What for?" said Earl.

Mason shook his head and held out his hand. Earl squatted. He slid a knife from his boot and passed it to him. Mason took the blade, turned the knife about in his hand. He walked to the body.

He knelt beside the corpse and pushed at the belly of the corpse with a hand. He slid the knife in just to one side of the outturned nombril. The blade went in smooth but fouled upon something within the man and slid away, Mason pushing it in hard until one corner of the hilt was lost and the handle skewed sideways and the tip of the blade poking almost through the man's side, its hard gray streak showing just under the skin. He brought the knife up and straightened the handle and pushed the knife down straight to the hilt. He twisted it down through the hardness until the hardness gave way.

He pulled the knife free. Fisting the stomach, he felt the air push out, the lips of the wound stammering, spattering the belly with blood.

He wiped the blade in the man's hair. Putting the knife down, he took up the shovel. He struggled to the hole. He started to scrape.

They put their shovels aside. Earl scraped the dust out of the hole. He paced the hole in even strides. He measured the height of the walls against his shovel, measured his shovel against the man.

"Think it will do him?" said Mason.

"Not in a coffin," said Earl. "Not alone neither," he said.

"They bringing a box?" said Mason.

Earl shrugged. "Said they were," he said.

"The fuckers," said Mason.

They set about the hole again, making lean progress.

"He's swelled up again," said Mason.

"Slit him," said Earl.

Mason stepped from the hole and gathered the knife. He bent down. He forced the knife into the hole of the belly. He sawed the blade upwards until the knife caught on the ribs and grated. He pushed down. The stomach grew puckered and loose.

"Think he got a full bladder?"

"Doubt it," said Mason.

"Any fluid in him?" said Earl.

"A little, must," said Mason.

"Drag him over," said Earl. "Put him to work."

They opened his veins, hacking into the joint of the elbow. With their thumbs they forced the blood up from the fingers and down from the shoulders. The fluid dripped out the elbow and into the hole, thick and coagulated. They opened the other elbow, then the veins of the neck. They gashed the back of the knees. They spread the blood around the hole with the back of the shovel blades, smoothing it evenly across the soil.

Stepping back, they wiped their shovel blades clean in the weeds. They watched the blood turn to paste.

"Haen't soaking in," said Mason.

"I haen't blind," said Earl.

They took their shovels to the hole, found the digging little easier. Earl threw down his shovel, got his knife up from the dirt. He turned the corpse over and rolled it onto its face and into the hole. When he turned it face up again, the face was daubed in blood.

He drew the zipper of the trousers all the way open. He hitched the trousers and the undergarments down until the hips were exposed, the hipbones rolling dull in flesh. He slit a line from one hipbone to the other. He slid one hand to the knuckle into the wound, prodding the organs beneath. His other hand insinuated the knife, pushed it deep, drew it across.

He pulled the body onto its side and pushed his hand into the wound. A pale stenched fluid rushed forth, pocked with clots. It slid the outcurve of the belly to spill across the hips, the pants soaking. He pushed again, harder. The fluid came faster.

They dragged the body from the hole. They spread the liquid around the hole and let it sink in, and dug out a crust of dirt.

Earl measured the sides of the hole against the shovel.

"Think it do him?" said Mason.

"Got to," said Earl.

They took the body up together. They carried it over to the hole and dropped it into the hole, the stiffened limbs arattle in striking the hard floor.

Earl came down on his knees. He turned his head, pressing the side of his face to the dirt.

"He don't fit," Earl said.

Mason nodded. He moved astraddle the hole. Lifting his shovel up above his head, he brought down the flat of it against the man's chest, the flesh smacking. He stepped and stood on the chest, striking his heels against the man's chest until the ribs collapsed and split through the sides, the chest folding in along the sternum. He stepped off, rubbed his boots clean in the weeds.

"Now?" said Mason, moving again astraddle the hole.

"Nope," said Earl. "Feet."

His brother rested the shovel blade against the ankle. He grunted, pushed the blade through gristle and bone, the foot shearing off dull and bloodless. He cut through the other foot, leaving both feet upturned and touching, jumbled between the terminal ankles.

"Well?" said Mason.

"Could have broke his legs and twisted the feet sidewards," Earl said.

Mason shrugged. "Could have," he said. "Well?"

"Nope," said Earl.

"The face, is it?" said Mason.

Earl nodded.

Mason stepped over, stepped into the hole, the curve of his boot rubbing the man's bare forearm. He squatted and reached out, tugging at the other's lower jaw, the jaw staying stiff, then of a sudden popping loose. He held down the chin with one hand, separating the dry lips with his other.

Standing, he rested the tip of the blade between the man's
lip and gum. He raised his foot, pushed the blade forward.

The lip stretched, split, tore free. The shovel pushed up
through the cartilage of the nose, the face shearing off whole
until the whole of it was loose and flapping and curled against
the shovel blade, the forehead wrinkling above.

He pulled the stripped flesh of the face back so it hung in a
swath over the scalp. He examined the face beneath the face,
the injured and frayed muscles of the jaw, the stripped sockets,
the shaved eyes.

He lifted the shovel, beat the face down, the teeth cracking
and rattling down into the throat.

They dragged over the man's shirt, rolling the clods and
platelets of dirt off it and down into the hole, atop and around
the man. The dirt lay across him in lumps, scattered uneven out
the sides of the hole. His body showed through the cracks.

"Don't look like a ten dollar burial," said Earl.

"Make water on him," said Mason.

"I'm dry as bone," said Earl.

He reached down and, pushing clods aside, took the man
by the wrist. He slid his hands under the arms, locked them
across the man's chest. He pulled him from the hole, tipped the
clods off him.

"Take his ankles," he said.

Mason dropped the shovel. He took the dead man by the
what was left of his ankles and together they pulled him off the
ground. They carried him around the back of the hill. They swung
him back and forth and let fall.

The body tumbled downslope, shivering each time it struck.

They returned to the hole. They pulled all the dirt they had
into it, stamped the empty grave back and forth. They sat down,
waited for the others to arrive.

They saw the minister's dark hat and the head of him, the rest
of the man to follow. They stood to greet him. They tucked the tails
of their shirts in and slid their shovels into the weeds, out of sight.

"Hey, Reverend," said Mason.

"Reverend," said Earl.

The Reverend rubbed his hands together, looking around him.

"Where's the body?" he said.

They pointed together to the mounded dirt.

"Sunk," said Mason.

"We buried him," said Earl.

"They already brought the coffin?" said the Reverend.

"Coffin?" said Mason.

"You didn't say anything about a coffin," said Earl.

"Jesus," said the Reverend. "This one has kin," he said, gesturing behind him to where they could see the hats already appearing. "Dig him up," he said.

"Seems a shame to dig one up," said Earl.

"A real shame," said Mason.

"More a shame when you don't get paid," said the Reverend. "Dig him up."

The kin had appeared to the waist, a younger and an elder, a pine coffin slung heavy between them. They reached the grave and put the pine coffin to one side of the grave, near where the Reverend continued to harangue the gravediggers. They wiped their faces. They rolled down their shirtsleeves and took brass cufflinks from their pockets and cuffed the sleeves of their shirts down. They buttoned the collars onto their shirts and knotted the cravats. They looked around, the Reverend and the gravediggers watching.

"Where is he?" the kin said.

Mason shrugged.

"We buried him," said Earl.

"Without the coffin?"

"Didn't hear nothing about a coffin," said Mason.

"What's Ma gone to say?" said the younger kin to the elder.

"Who the hell's Ma?" said Mason.

"Shut up, Mason," said Earl.

The Reverend had already come to the kin and was holding his hands as if to encircle them.

"Earl and Mason here will dig him up," he said. "They will bury him right. You will see."

"The hell we are," said Mason.

"Shut up, Mason," said Earl.

"Don't pay them until you have your satisfaction," said the Reverend.

"Got to pay us," said Mason.

"The hell they do," said the Reverend. "Don't pay them."

"Dig him yourselves," said Mason.

"You hired this pair?" said the elder of the kin.

"There is nobody else," said the Reverend. "They never gave me trouble before."

"Always a first time," said the elder.

"Don't pay them until they do it right," said the Reverend.

"Why don't you go down by the river," said the elder.

"The river?" said the Reverend.

"Wait for us to call out," said the elder. "We will call for you."

The gravediggers watched the Reverend walk slowly down the slope of the hill, holding his hat with one hand, the other fluttering out to steady him against the slope. The elder kin turned.

"You two dig him up," he said.

"He's happy in the ground," said Mason.

"Ma's got to see him yet," said the younger kin.

"He's in a sorry state," said Earl. "She don't want to see him."

The other two shrugged in unison. The eldest nodded and the other man went to the pine coffin. He lifted the lid off and reached in, bringing out a double-barreled shotgun. He carried it to the eldest who broke open the breach and reached two shells out of his pocket. He loaded the shotgun, closed it, hung it in the crook of his arm.

"Wouldn't bury a man without his shotgun, would you?" he said.

The gravediggers regarded each other, but did not speak.

The man raised the shotgun, sighted it at Mason, at Earl.

"Would you?" he said.

They shook their heads. They gathered their shovels.

"Good," said the eldest. "I thought we might come to right a understanding."

They began to spade away the dirt.

"What we gone to do?" said Mason.

"Just keep digging," said Earl. "Just dig."

They hit the last of the loose earth and struck hardpan. They kept digging.

The eldest of the kin leaned over the hole and looked in. He leaned back, cocked the rifle.

"I don't believe he's in here," he said.

"He's in here," said Earl. "Just a little more."

They kept digging. It was tough going. The sky turned pale, darkened. They dug until the hole was deep enough to hold two bodies, and dug further, and kept digging.

Body

I. Body

I have been privately removed to St. Sebastian's Correctional Facility and Haven for the Wayward, where they are fitting me for a new mind, and body too. Most of my distress, they believe, results from having a wayward body and no knowledge of how to manage it. As mine is a body which does not sit easy with the world, they have chosen to begin again from scratch.

The body, says Brother Johanssen, *is not simple flesh staunching blood and slung over bones, but a way of slipping and spilling through the world.* While others slip like water through the world, I am always bottling the world up. The only way I can come unbottled is to crack the world apart. *One cannot refashion flesh and blood*, Brother Johanssen tells me, *but one can refashion the paths that flesh and blood take through the world.*

In a way you can remake the flesh and blood too, whispers Skarmus, *or unmake it, as you know, dear boy.* It is late one midnight, and I lie bound to the slab. I have no answer to this. His fingers are pushing through my hair. In the dark, I hear the grim smile in his voice. *That you hear what others see,* Brother Johanssen tells me, *is but further index of your illness.*

It is true, as Skarmus says, that I have acquired a certain skill at unmaking flesh and blood, dividing it and sectioning it into new creatures and forms as a means of transforming the distress of my wayward body into pleasure. Put into the brothers' terms, the only commerce I can stomach is with the dead. In a little time, I know to work away my distress by transforming another into a stripped- and lopped-off dark lump of flies. They do not know all of this, though they surely suspect. For what they do know, I am conscripted in Saint Sebastian's, subject to all things as I prepare to take up another, purer body.

Four buildings, four stations, four doors. Before I may enter any station, I am required to salute the doorframe of the remaining three. First lintel, then post, then lintel again, addressed in such fashion first with my right mitt, then with my left, then my body must spin sharply and stride to the next door.

Skarmus is with me as my private demon, tasked by the brothers to insure I meet all prescription regarding motion, that I salute door frames in proper order and fashion, that I locomote as they would have me do. I am to be impeded and interrupted by him. All is an effort and the brothers' belief is that my mind in the face of that effort must opt for the construction of another body.

There must, for reasons never explained to me, be an interval of five seconds between each gesture, no more, no less. I must regulate seconds as Skarmus challenges me with hands and voice. When my movements are irregular, the intervals inexact, I am forced to begin again. If I fail a second time, Skarmus is allowed to tighten the flap over my mouth until I can barely respire and slowly lose consciousness.

I cannot know if at night Skarmus whispers his own opinions or if his words are part of the brothers' larger plan for me. I attempt not to respond to his whispers or actions, attempt as far as possible to ignore Skarmus and coax him off guard. I have twice, despite the padded restraints engaging my hands and feet, despite the system wiring my jaw closed, beaten Skarmus sense-less. Indeed, I would have beaten him dead and attempted, de-spite my restraints, commerce with what was left of him, had not the brothers rapidly intervened.

Four stations, then, as follows: the Living, the Instruction, the Restriction, the Resurrection. I have entered all stations save the Resurrection. Here, Brother Johanssen believes, I am not yet prepared to go.

The Living: I am strapped flat around chest, wrists, ankles, throat. The mask is undone and set aside, the lights extinguished. I am allowed to sleep if I can so manage with Skarmus mum-bling over me.

At some point, lights flash on. A tube is forced between the wires encasing my mouth and I am fed.

Brother Johanssen arrives, the jawscrews are loosened, I am allowed a moment of untrammeled expression.

"How are you, brother?" Brother Johanssen asks. "Are you uncovering a new body within your skin?"

"I have a new body," I tell him. "I am utterly changed. I have given up evil and become a purely normal fellow."

He shakes his head, smiling thinly. "You believe me so gull-ible?" he asks. He makes a gesture and the jawscrews are tight-ened down, the mask re-initiated.

You must learn to deceive him, whispers Skarmus. *You must master better the art of the lie.*

Then we are up and outside and walking. The weights and baffles and mitts, always varied slightly from one day to the next. The restrictions, Skarmus' constant tug and thrust as I walk. My body remains aching and sore, unsure on its feet.

Skarmus is beside me, a half pace behind. Brother Johanssen is somewhere behind, out of sight, the other brothers as well. I am at the center of a world whose sole purpose is to circle about me.

The Instruction: I am made to listen to Brother Johanssen, Skarmus still whispering in my ear. *That which is wayward must be angled forward, the body surrendered for another*, Brother Johanssen preaches. I have, I am told, been wandering all the years of my life in the darkness of my imperfect body. Only the brothers can bring me into light.

You cannot be brought into the so-called light, whispers Skarmus. *You shall never survive it. For you there is no so-called light but only so-called darkness.*

I fail to understand the role of Skarmus. He seems intent on undoing all that Brother Johanssen attempts. Together, it is as if they are trying to tear me apart.

The beauty of the world, Brother Johanssen is saying, *objective, impersonal. For a body such as that which you still persist in wearing, an affront. Affreux. You must acquire a body which will live with beauty rather than against it.*

There is only against, states Skarmus.

The Restriction: when I am inattentive, when I resist, when I follow Skarmus' advice rather than that of the good brother, when I fail in my tasks and motions. The mask is tightened almost to suffocation, the flaps zipped down to block my ears, eyes, nose, the hands chained and dragged up above the head. The back of the rubber suit is loosened, parted, a range of sensations scattered over it or into it by devices I cannot perceive. At some point sweat begins to crease my back, or perhaps welts and blood.

It all revolves around not knowing. I cannot say if it is pain or pleasure I feel, the line between the two so easily traversable in the artificial distance from my own flesh. The dull thud coming distanced through my blocked ears, the flash of sensation flung across the skull at first and then barely perceptible, the damp smell within the leather mask.

"How are you, brother?" Brother Johanssen asks. "Have you found your new body?"

"I have a new body now, dear brother," I say. I strain against the straps. "I am a changed man."

He shakes his finger back and forth over me slowly. "I see you take me for a fool," he says.

A brief flash through the stations, a day in the space of a moment, my mind at some distance from my body and the light goes off. I feel fingers in my hair. *You cannot believe any of this*, Skarmus says. *You must not allow them to take away what you are.*

Lintel, post, lintel with right. Lintel, post, lintel with left. The muffled blows the mitt offers with each strike.

A slow turn, the foot coming up. Stumbling to the next door, Skarmus clinging to one of my legs.

"You are not prepared for the Resurrection," says Brother Johanssen, leaning benevolently over me.

You'll never be ready, Skarmus whispers.

The chains tighten. I feel my back stripped bare. In the darkness inside my mask, I see streaks of light.

I open my mouth to speak. They are already screwing my jaw down.

A remembered ruin of bodies and myself panting among them, yet with no complete memory of having taken them apart.

I am different from anyone else in the world.

He is smiling, waiting for me to speak. I close my eyes. He pries them open, waits, waits. Finally lets them go, tightens the jawscrews down until my teeth ache and grate.

Skarmus falls slightly ahead of me and for a moment I feel myself and my body clearly my own again. He stumbles and I have my mitts on either side of his head and am holding his head still as I strike through it with my own masked head, as I lift him up to bring the side of his skull down against my muffled knee. Were I not so restrained and softened by padding he would be dead. As it is, it is a sort of awkward game.

I try to snap his head to one side and break his neck but the mitts give slightly and the neck groans but refuses to snap. There is a flurry of bodies and Skarmus is dragged away and other hands are holding me down, pulling the mask off, holding my own head down. I see the brief glint of the long needle, feel it pricked into my skull, just above the rim of my eye.

"An inch more," says Brother Johanssen. "A simple rotation of the wrist, brother, and you shall have little relation to any body at all. Is that what you choose?"

I move my eyes no, feel the pressure of the needle.

"Are you telling me that all our time has been wasted?" He looks at me long, without expression, the needle an everpresent pressure, a red blot now drawing itself into my vision. "It is too late for a full cure," says Brother Johanssen. "Your body is too stubborn in its ways. We can redirect it but slightly."

Brother Johanssen gestures and I feel the needle slick back out, see it fluxed and dripping blood, moving away. There lies Skarmus, his jaw blistered black and blue. He is silent for once.

"The Resurrection then," says Brother Johanssen as blood curls over my eye. "This is all we can do. May God forgive us."

II. Shoe

In the polished ceiling of the Living, in the few moments I have free of the mask, I see the flesh above my eye gone dark and turgid, swelling like a second eye. Below it the original eye wavers and falls dim. In a few awakenings its vision is altogether gone, the enormous fist of death beginning to open in its place.

They sedate me and scrape the eye from the socket and drain the ichor from it and scald the socket clean. Skarmus speaks muffled, morphined, his jaw wrapped, his voice mumbled.

I was right, he means to say. *I was right all along*.

His gestures of impediment have subsided, seem half-hearted at best. I am allowed to touch each doorframe largely unimpeded, move in my wires and chains into the Resurrection at last.

It is a simple station, a single room, a low light in the center of it. Brother Johanssen is already there, waiting, at attention, his simple garments exchanged for brighter brocaded robes.

I am made to sit. I am then strapped in place and into a head-brace locked so I am forced to regard him.

"These are the initial terms of the Resurrection," he says.

Top Lift
Eyelet
Aglet
Grommet
Vamp

He holds it up, cupped in his hand. He displays it in the light.

"Do you see the curve here?" asks Brother Johanssen a few sessions later, tracing along the side. "Employ your imagination. What does it conjure up?"

They are trying to change you, whispers Skarmus.

"On a woman's body, brother. What does it recall?"

He brings it close, traces the curves, holds it close to my face, describes the minor shadings and traces. When I close my eyes, Brother Johanssen commands Skarmus to hold them open, both of them, the missing and the whole. He is touching the shoe, caressing it, speaking still in a way that makes the shoe steam and glimmer, glister in the odd light as if threatening to become something else.

Quarter, he says.

Cuff.

Counter.

Heel.

When I wake he is there, leaning over me, my jaw already screwed open. "Do you accept the fruits of your new faith?" he asks.

"What?" I say.

"What?" he says. He stands and begins to weave away. "What?" he repeats, "What?"

Throat, someone says behind me.

Tongue, someone says.

He dims the central light, disappears himself somewhere behind me. A square of light as big as myself appears, flashes onto the wall before me.

You are in it, says Skarmus. *Too late to step back now.*

The square of light goes dark, is exchanged for the image of the forepart of a woman's shoe, the dip between the first and

second toe captured in the low cleft of the vamp. It flashes away
and is replaced by pallid white flesh, the dip of a dress, the slow
curve and fall of the woman's body.

There may be a resemblance, says Skarmus. *Yet it is entirely
superficial.*

The images are flashed back and forth, one replacing the
other soon with such speed it becomes difficult to know where
one image stops, the other begins.

Breast, someone says.

Cleave.

Box.

I hear the clatter behind me, the square of light pulsing and
then a shoe fading up and angling in and transforming into a
woman. Then the shoe again and a different place, followed by
a section of the woman. The clatter, swirling motes of dust bright
in the beam of light.

It is her breast, its breast, her feet, its foot, her neck and
shoulder, its neck and shoulder, cleave, cleave, thigh, thigh, box,
box, counter, counter, welt, welt, looping to begin all over again.

Skarmus is speaking filth into my ear.

The film is sped double time, looped over and over. In my
good eye I am seeing the parsed shoe, in my missing eye the
parsed woman. At some point there stops being a difference.

Sole.

I feel his hands through my hair. I test my bonds, find them
tight.

Every shoe was once a woman, he says. *A shoe is a woman
in a new body. There is, for your purpose, no distinction.*

Welt, he whispers. *Box.*

When I open my eye there is a flash of gold, pendulant,
turning back and forth above me. I try to lift my head but cannot
lift it. I do not feel the pressure of the jawscrew, yet my jaw will
not move.

There is the steady sweep of Brother Johanssen's voice, speaking slowly and calmly and with authority, his body invisible except, above the flush of gold, a pale and disembodied hand.
Skarmus is nowhere to be seen or heard.

His cadence changes, his words coming slower, matching the rhythm of the swinging gold. "One," he intones. "Two. Thr—"

I have lately been experiencing some uncertainty as to who I am and where and when. I am becoming strange to myself, caught somehow outside my own skin.

I hear a noise like the snap of a bone.

I am in the Resurrection, not knowing how I have come to be here. The padding and restrictions have been removed from my arms and instead I hold in my hands the subject of all my time in the Resurrection.

I stand still, holding it, observing it. I begin to stroke softly, my heart beating harder, until I feel my arms overwhelmed by other hands and the object is falling out of my hands, and I am crying out into the closed surface of a mask.

The mouth flap is tightened, and I feel the breath slowly leaving me. The baffles are fitted over my hands. Brother Johanssen moves until I can see him through the eyelets of the mask. He is smiling. He has picked the subject up, holds it suspended from a single finger, swaying, near my face.

"Dear brother," he says, leaning forward as my air gives out. "Welcome to the fold."

They hold me down and in place and strip all the apparatuses from me piece by piece until I am bare and shivering and in a heap on the ground, lost without the sweat and smell of baffles and rubber and leather and wire. They carry me by the arms and legs, toss me. There is the moment of collision with the floor, a sensation more naked and complete than anything I have felt in some time.

As I am getting up, stumbling in my body, I hear the sound of the door snapping to.

I can barely walk, the ground wavering under my feet.

I am, I know, in the Resurrection. In the cast light, centered, a woman of red leather, sleek and low cut, satined inside, without eyelets, aglets, grommets, perhaps twelve inches from heel to toe box. She is lovely, her shank perfectly curved, needle heeled, her vamp v-shaped and elongated.

I am moving forward. I reach and pick her up in my hand, touch her against my long-encased skin.

After that I cannot explain what happens. There is a rush of dizziness and when I awake she is destroyed, strips of leather and thin wood and metal are scattered about, her heel broken off and free. There is, as always, tremendous regret and shame.

I turn to see Brother Johanssen and Skarmus together, complicitous in the doorway. I lift my shoulders, try to think of something to say. Then the door opens and all the brothers are upon me in a rush, ladening me down, binding me again.

Each day I am stripped to my skin, left alone with her. I may, Brother Johanssen tells me, remain with her as long as I do not destroy her.

I do what I can to resist. I make conversation. I resist, for a time, touching her. When I do touch her it is merely slightly, turning her, attempting to perceive, briefly, a new aspect. I let things build slowly, but in the end am always lying spent, strips and fragments of her scattered about me.

Yet each day she is there again, the same, velvet on the outside, silken innards. I can destroy her, but she keeps returning. It is, after all, the Resurrection.

That's right, says Skarmus. *Keep destroying it*.
It? I wonder.

The film gets stuck. I watch the image darken, bloom black and dissolve into light. I am not the only one who destroys.

There is some confusion in me about who I am, what I desire.

I keep destroying her. I am not changed, my body just as wayward as ever. Yet they are happier with me. I understand none of it.

Then I am stripped and thrown in again, as if to the lions. Yet this time there is no woman, only an odd and curious creature, the same size as myself, much like myself, only not a man. It grimaces, brushes back its hair. It is all familiar somehow.

"This is your body's test," says Brother Johanssen. "Do not fail us."

I do not know what is expected of me. I approach slowly. It makes no move, seems at ease, relaxed. It begins to mumble words that I can't quite string together.

Breast, throat, quarter. Suddenly I can see the woman hidden in it, luminous, the leather and satin cached just beneath hair and teeth and skin.

Through her skin I brush her vamp, finger the damp welt. They cannot conceal her from me in such a carapace. In a minute, I know, I will have shucked the carapace and she will be strips of leather, her box torn apart and open, her throat undone, all of her gone.

The Installation
_____

The gray square above is meant to stand in for a photograph of my dead wife, may she rest in peace. For a photograph, that is, of my wife dead and in her coffin, which I took during the first moments of the memorial service before my presence was detected and I was forced to flee. Were the image actually present, you would see how carefully the undertaker has worked to make her other than she is. The color her flesh here appears to be reveals nothing of the gray pallor which afflicted her body as she approached death. In place of the carefully waved wig here depicted, her hair had been coming out in clumps, her scalp spasmed with red sores. Her hands, formerly gnarled and clenched, are here spread flat one atop the other on her belly. I know from the undertaker that this last effect was achieved only by breaking the fingers after death with a pair of pliers. The quality of the film I employed was sufficiently high that, with the aid of a magnifying glass, one can make out beneath the powder the plier's scoring on the skin of her joints.

This gray square is meant to be seen as chronologically following the first photograph, though in point of fact it was taken before. With the help of the undertaker, whose assistance was secured through a modest remuneration, I made a face for my wife while she lay spread upon the metal table in the private portion of the mortuary. Her lips are grotesque, like the mouth of a clown. Her eyelids are pushed open and the eyes independently rolled in opposite directions, giving her an amphibial gaze. Her wig is on but loose, pulled askew. One hand is gnarled and curled while the other, joints already broken, lies flat and smooth.

There were other things I intended to do with the body, but the undertaker's infectious nervousness prevented me. And perhaps just as well, for as it was I was nearly discovered by my wife's family, by my wife's father, who unexpectedly appeared. Luckily there was sufficient time to hide me on another metal table under a shroud and to throw a folded shroud over my dead wife's face. My father-in-law noticed nothing.

My wife had always been a patron of the arts, and as such understood my work a great deal better than her relations did. My wife and I met at the Kalsteiner Museum, at a photography exhibit to which I had contributed one of my works, "Living Room": hundreds of death masks arranged to completely cover all the available surface of a room. I was standing near my photograph, at a slight distance, observing people's reactions, when she stopped in front of it. She was, in those days, quite lovely, her skin suffused with a color not unlike that seen in the photograph of her in her coffin, discussed above. Her hair was intact and pulled back tightly against her head, bound in the back by a clip. Her fingers were impeccably manicured. I do not recall what she was wearing, though I am certainly not incapable of making something up, as I will surely have to do if the installation is to be completed in the way I intend.

The installation will consist of a single square room, accessible through a hole cut in the North wall near the floor. To enter, one must crawl on hands and knees. The only light will come from narrow slits cut near the ceiling. In the center of the installation will be my wife's casket, open, with or without the body depending upon whether the courts (assuming the issue ever comes to court) uphold my appeal. If they do not, then a replica of my wife's casket. I should state that if I am allowed the body, I am willing to seal it in some way, bowing to the demands of etiquette and sanitation. Though an artist, I am also a reasonable man.

The third photograph, moving down the East wall, was taken shortly before the second but is meant, chronologically, to appear later. In it, half of my wife's face is garishly painted as per the second photograph. The other half is collapsed and gray, its eye closed, lips pale. It is as if death is spreading itself into her, slipping from right to left, a foreign reader.

In the Kalsteiner Museum, I observed her for some time before finally approaching her.

"Do you like it?" I asked.

"Yes," she said. "Very much."

"I know the artist," I said.

"Is that so?"

"Would you be interested in meeting him?"

"Why not," she said.

I bowed slightly to her. "Mademoiselle," I said. "He is at your service."

There is no truth to her family's accusations that when she married me she was unaware of my art, of the nature of it. Admittedly at first she thought the death masks were simply plaster casts of the faces of the living, but I quickly disabused her of that notion, tutoring her in my ideas and techniques. Yet, her family continues to insist on two falsities: first, that she had no awareness of my art until well after the marriage; second, that she had never been either to the Kalsteiner Museum or even to Kalsteinberg at all.

I have, as an act of good faith, placed several captioned snapshots in the Kalsteinberg paper, asking for anyone who might have seen my wife and me on that day to come forward. So far, none have come forward. Largely, I suspect, because anyone likely to have gone to that particular exhibit would read the Berlin papers rather than the local Kalsteinberg rag.

I can testify that my relationship with my wife during the approximately six months of our marriage was a good one. Our relationship was never strained, even once she fell ill, which she quickly did. If, as her parents allege, I kept them away from their daughter it was from her own wishes, because she didn't want to see them, for three reasons. First, she did not want her parents to see her in her diseased state. Second, she despised her parents and had for a long time wanted to cut herself off from them. Finally, we had already engaged on the project which I saw as the culmination of my life's work and which she saw as the culmination of her existence. Engaged seriously in the work, she wanted no distractions.

The three gray squares above indicate a triptych of photographs that will dominate the south wall of the installation. They are placed in the middle of the wall on a six-foot tall rectangular sheet of anodized aluminum meant vaguely to suggest a door. There may in fact be two triptychs, one atop the other, but until I have my photographs back from my wife's family, I cannot be certain.

In each photograph, the camera has been placed in the same spot and is directed at the same angle. Each photograph is shot at the same time of day, in morning light. At the left of the shot one can see the corner of the window, a thin and soft angle of light bleeding through at the edge. To the right, the pole of a lamp and the lower edge of its illuminated shade. Between the two, in each and every photograph, my wife lies in her bed.

The triptych will chronicle her illness, the 74 days from the time she first fell ill to when she died, but will do so in reverse: the first picture, chosen from the last days of her illness, shows her cheeks collapsed, her face wrinkled, her hair gone. In the second, she is less devastated, her hair thinning but largely intact. The last picture shows her nearly healthy, serene in sleep, ready to awaken refreshed to meet the day.

Each day of her long decline, I arose early, breakfasted, showered. At 7 a.m. precisely I took her photograph, first adjusting her head slightly to face the lamp in a fashion close, if not quite identical, to how it had faced the lamp in the photograph of the day before. I ask you, if my wife had not been fully supportive of my project, would she have allowed me day after day to arrange her head, and would she have been willing to hold it in place for the time it took to take the photograph?

If there is a second triptych below, it will consist of three photographs from the middle of my wife's illness, three consecutive photographs in which no change in my wife's condition is revealed or in which the change revealed is slight, only perceptible after careful attention to the sequence. Conceptually speaking, I am not yet certain if such an image of stasis will further or thwart the aim of the installation as a whole.

I had, of course, proper permission to photograph first my wife and then my wife's corpse in the fashion I did. A reputable lawyer drew up a document in which my wife made her intentions perfectly clear. She signed it as well—though according to her family the signature is wrong, is not her signature. I, unfortunately, did not have the foresight to provide for a witness or notary, yet nevertheless I was still astonished when a judge chose to agree with the family. Thus was set into motion the process by which I lost all my photographs, not to mention my other memorabilia, all of which was crucial to my artistic project.

My wife was ill. When one is ill, particularly to the degree my wife was ill, one's signature changes. Consider again her hands, how gnarled they had become. How could she be expected to grasp the pen as she once had, back in the days when her hands were unblemished and smooth.

And even had I signed it, I would have done so only at her request. I am an ethical man. I would never force a stranger, let alone someone close to me, let alone my wife, to do something against their will. The signature should be considered binding.

On the west wall, a photograph of a 1" section of her bare scalp, magnified and reproduced several thousand times, each photograph aligned carefully against the next to create a square that covers the majority of the wall. In the center of the square, at eye level, a small anodized aluminum shelf upon which is the hair I collected off her brush each morning. Hair which, near the end, came off in clumps if I simply brushed my palm along her head. Her hair is woven into a loose rope, waxed slightly to keep stray strands in place. Perhaps I will arrange it into some pattern. Beside it, a small glass vial containing her nail clippings and flakes of her skin. Beside that, a simple discolored but empty vial, plain and featureless, a label scratched off it.

It is true that her father had said, as he reiterated at the injunction hearing, that he thought our wedding "precipitous." True, we were married shortly after we met; true, that marriage was in some senses sudden; true, in retrospect her parents had perhaps been hurt by not being allowed to meet me until the wedding day just a few moments before the ceremony. But weddings are always in a sense precipitous, parents always in a sense hurt. Besides, it was not me but my wife who pushed for a quick wedding, and it was she who chose to keep her parents away from me until the last possible moment—knowing as she did that her parents had despised all the men of her past and had broken up every one of her relationships.

In addition, I suspect now as well that one reason she pushed for a rapid wedding was because she knew or sensed that she was already afflicted with the still-undiagnosed illness that would kill her. Perhaps she wanted a few months of relative health and happy marriage before her illness became too much for her to ignore. If my suspicions are correct, then if anyone was manipulating anyone, she was manipulating me.

The fact that I am in hiding now should not be read as an indication of my guilt—only as an acknowledgment of the power and relentlessness of her wealthy parents, and as an awareness of the corruption of the justice system. I am not guilty, but I am also not a fool. Nor should the fact that the place where I am hiding resembles to no little degree the imagined space of my installation be seen as an indication that my art has, suddenly, taken a mimetic turn.

The only exit is the same as the entrance, the low hole in the wall that one must crawl through on hands and knees. Ideally, sufficient numbers will visit the installation that there will be a constant struggle between people coming in and people going out, with eight to ten people crammed claustrophobically into the small room at any given moment. The coffin or the coffin's replica must be positioned to allow only a fairly narrow space for viewers to walk between it and the four walls. Ideally, the spectator should find it difficult to establish any distance from the images on the walls.

At night, I crawl out the hole in the back. I purchase comestibles and batteries at a convenience store, furtively, and then return to walk about with a flashlight. I shine the light, turning the names over in my mouth, but my wife's name is nowhere to be found.

According to her parents, my wife had objections to my art the whole way along. In fact, she had no objections—or at least if she did she did not voice them to me. My suspicion is that any objection she voiced before her parents was a concession to them, that they imposed their views on her and out of politeness or nervousness or simple cravenness she chose not to argue.

In any case, even if she had objections, she must have given them entirely up as her life approached its end. She spoke, when able to speak at all, in glowing terms of my work and her role in it. Her own approach to death led her to a full understanding of my work.

There are, of course, the photographs that will not be included in the installation, thousands of them, taken in the three days after my wife's death. I have come to understand that the public will certainly shy away from these later images—which, in addition, I know for a fact my in-laws have destroyed. Perhaps the other photographs I have discussed are destroyed as well, the rope of hair burnt, and I will have to begin again, with another subject, another wife.

Her family was exceptionally angered that I did not call a doctor directly after her death, that I instead began manipulating the body, taking pictures. But that was the agreement between us, her wish as well as my own. Besides, what point in calling a doctor to administer to a dead woman? And whatever one's feelings about the doctor, it must have been clear to them from the character of the air in the house in the instant after forcing my front door open that there was no longer any need of a doctor. Knowing this, they should not have climbed the stairs and forced the bedroom door open—had they merely knocked I might have covered the body, gathered myself, done whatever I could to lessen the blow. Had they not discovered their daughter in a full and unadulterated confrontation with her death, and myself in the full swing of the next stage of my art, surprising even myself—perhaps then I might have been able to talk some sense into them. As it was, the only interaction I received from her father, hardly a connoisseur of the arts, was a severe beating. But said beating was a blessing in the end, for had it been a little less severe and not led to my defenestration into the bushes below the bedroom, I certainly would not have managed to effect a departure before the police arrived.

I try to keep in mind that art has always faced such setbacks but that, as the history of art has shown, in the end it always triumphs. Whether the installation takes place or not, I have learned enough from the process to know what paths to pursue. It is up to the world to follow me.

Nor do I suspect that my wife and I have seen the last of each other. I have made a few well-placed inquiries. I am on her trail again. Our collaboration, I suspect, has only just begun.

Garker's Aestheticals

I.

It were a word. It name were God.

It gangled my tongue. It were crawed up my throat. Word God were given me the choke.

Spatted it out all about the crackwood floor. Luppen and lappen it up all from the crackwood floor. Gangled it trussed with my mean slivered tongue.

Pulped it pasty atween my molar teeth. Gave it the swallow, did I. Word went down smooth, did it. There were mouthwater to helpen it down. There were a swaller of nonesuch to helpen it down.

I frittered and setted about in some chairs. Stomach all gone achurn. Stomach were getten to got me up, given me the nudge for haven a spew. Took the spoon to the throat. Nothing come up. Looken way down my proper throat in the glass. Nothing done it to be sawn save the mean slivered tongue.

The guts on me wrought pain. It were fallen to the floor, for me. It were not gotten up, for me. Just the dry shake.

I shucked off the clothes.

I nuded there cold, shuddered in darkly.

II.

The sun were burnen the awful upsky course. The crackwood were all shite-ran to stank.

It were me the culprit. God were pointen the finger.

I scribed in my wastefuls upon floor, wall. I were thought to scribe upon my own bodywise, which I done. I sprent myself shitely.

III.

Night come on by. Men come on by. They getten their gander up with the most of it. They shored up the nostril for the stank.

Runnen the crackwood with shite were no proper etiquette, it were suggested me.

I weren't said none to answer.

They were got me by the limbses. I given nary a kick.

They pucked me up out of the miry bowel. I don't gatten no struggle still in me, don't done none with me. They went, carried me from the miry bowel.

But I were the last laugh, were I. I were it, I were. I were astank all to my way to my high heaven.